P9-CQH-639

Buffy was swinging, jumping, defying some gravity, when she noticed the little demon guy hovering at the end of the alley.

This time he wore blue, the color this batch of demons favored, but he still had the same symbol on his robes.

This moment of distraction cost her. A wide noose slipped over her neck and down past her shoulders. It pinned her arms to her side as it was pulled taut, and hauled her straight up a dozen feet.

The demoness at the other end of the rope smiled. Perfect teeth, too.

Evil, pure evil.

Buffy was trying to find a way to free herself when the demoness swung her *hard*. Suddenly, the wall was rushing toward her, ready to swat her like a bug even though she'd never done anything to it.

Buffy squeezed her eyes shut.

*This* was gonna hurt.

## Buffy the Vampire Slayer™

Buffy the Vampire Slayer
    (movie tie-in)
The Harvest
Halloween Rain
Coyote Moon
Night of the Living Rerun
Blooded
Visitors
Unnatural Selection
The Power of Persuasion
Deep Water
Here Be Monsters
Ghoul Trouble
Doomsday Deck
Sweet Sixteen
The Angel Chronicles, Vol. 1

The Angel Chronicles, Vol. 2
The Angel Chronicles, Vol. 3
The Xander Years, Vol. 1
The Xander Years, Vol. 2
The Willow Files, Vol. 1
The Willow Files, Vol. 2
How I Survived My Summer Vacation,
    Vol. 1
The Faith Trials, Vol. 1
Tales of the Slayer, Vol. 1
The Lost Slayer serial novel
    Part 1: Prophecies
    Part 2: Dark Times
    Part 3: King of the Dead
    Part 4: Original Sins

## Available from ARCHWAY Paperbacks and POCKET PULSE

Child of the Hunt
Return to Chaos
The Gatekeeper Trilogy
    Book 1: Out of the Madhouse
    Book 2: Ghost Roads
    Book 3: Sons of Entropy
Obsidian Fate
Immortal
Sins of the Father

Resurrecting Ravana
Prime Evil
The Evil That Men Do
Paleo
Spike and Dru: Pretty Maids
    All in a Row
Revenant
The Book of Fours
The Unseen Trilogy (Buffy/Angel)
    Book 1: The Burning
    Book 2: Door to Alternity
    Book 3: Long Way Home

The Watcher's Guide, Vol. 1: The Official Companion to the Hit Show
The Watcher's Guide, Vol. 2: The Official Companion to the Hit Show
The Postcards
The Essential Angel
The Sunnydale High Yearbook
Pop Quiz: Buffy the Vampire Slayer
The Monster Book
The Script Book, Season One, Vol. 1
The Script Book, Season One, Vol. 2
The Script Book, Season Two, Vol. 1
The Script Book, Season Two, Vol. 2

Available from POCKET BOOKS

# SWEET SIXTEEN

## Scott Ciencin

**An original novel based on the hit television series
by Joss Whedon**

SIMON PULSE

NEW YORK  LONDON  TORONTO  SYDNEY  SINGAPORE

If you purchased this book without a cover, you should be aware that this book is stolen property. It was reported as "unsold and destroyed" to the publisher and neither the author nor the publisher has received any payment for this "stripped book."

This book is a work of fiction. Any references to historical events, real people, or real locales are used fictitiously. Other names, characters, places, and incidents are the product of the author's imagination and any resemblance to actual events or locales or persons, living or dead, is entirely coincidental.

First Simon Pulse edition April 2002

™ and © 2002 Twentieth Century Fox Film Corporation.
All rights reserved.

SIMON PULSE
An imprint of Simon & Schuster
Children's Publishing Division
1230 Avenue of the Americas
New York, NY 10020

All rights reserved, including the right of
reproduction in whole or in part in any form.

The text of this book was set in Times.
Printed in the United States of America.
2 4 6 8 10 9 7 5 3 1
Library of Congress Catalog Card Number: 2001098567
ISBN: 0-7434-2732-7

For my eternal love Denise.

# Acknowledgments:

Special thanks to Lisa Clancy, Micol Ostow, and Liz Shiflett of Pocket Books, author Jeff Mariotte, and Joss Whedon, David Greenwalt, Amy McIntyre Britt, and all the talented creators, crew, and cast of the best show on television.

# Chapter One

Tentacles writhed under the dark leather coat of the man ahead of Buffy. She knew they were tentacles because of the slimy tips poking out from the coat's wide sleeves. The slippery puddle of goo this guy and his three buddies left wherever they shuffled was another dead giveaway they were out-of-towners.

Buffy readied herself for a fight. It was two in the morning, and the Slayer stood in line at the Quick Stop, waiting to pay for the cereal she'd picked up so Dawn wouldn't go hungry in the morning—not that her little sister ever ate anything that was good for her anyway— and a Twinkie.

All *she'd* wanted was a Twinkie. A harmless Twinkie. You would *think* harmless.

Tell that to Tentacle Guy.

Buffy surveyed the potential battlefield. Okay, harsh overhead lighting, lots of narrow aisles, a double glass door entrance at the front, big glass windows looking onto a practically deserted parking lot and gas pumps, a hall leading to bathrooms, an office, a supply room or two, and an exit in the back. Two civilians, the bleary eyed carrot-topped teen at the cash register talking away on his cell phone, and a tall, scraggly-haired blond girl about Dawn's age wearing a dark oversized sweatshirt and jeans against the far wall, grabbing things from the freezer. Round mirrors were positioned in every corner to help Buffy have eyes in the back of her head during a fight, but there were also surveillance cameras and monitors.

*Better to get this out into the parking lot,* away from prying video cameras. Better still to get it into that open field local developers had been promising for years to turn into a strip mall. But she had plenty of weapons on her if the uglies got ugly here in the store, and if she needed to improvise, there were lots of heavy cans that could be used for beaning monsters, and aerosols, lighter fluids, cleaning chemicals, and more—all the ingredients for a late-night monster meat cookout.

Outfit wise, she was fine for fighting. A beige turtleneck sweater under a short, dark brown leather jacket. Matching spandex-tight boot-cut pants, and shiny high-heeled boots. She could move in these clothes like they were a second skin.

She tensed, waiting for the closest creature to make a move—then noticed the big sack of cat food Tentacle Guy was carrying. The cutest little *meow* came from one of his deep pockets, and a furry little head with two bright inquisitive eyes popped up.

*I tought I taw a putty-tat!*

Running her hand over her forehead, Buffy wondered if the long nights were finally getting to her. Still, the most threatening thing this guy had done so far was exist, and she couldn't go after him for that.

A tentacle reached out and stroked the head of the brown and orange furred kitten.

"Good Pumpkin," a deep, throaty voice rumbled. "Nice-nice."

The kitten purred and hummed as the tentacle stroked her silky head. Sounding just like a tiny motor turning over, she contentedly slid down into the pocket. *Well, this is new. Tentacle Guy is a member of Pet-Loving Fiends. Maybe this was going to work out after all. . . .*

Tentacle Guy slapped the bag of cat food onto the counter while his buddies congregated near the door. They were all hooded, but, considering the way it had been cold and raining and everything, Buffy hadn't made anything of that. Now she glanced in their direction, scanning the odd shapes inside the hoods where human features would have been—if these guys had been human.

Carrot-top didn't look up into the face of his customer. He was still all gabby with his cell phone. "Can't wait to get off tonight, gonna quit this job, get out of this town, finally be free for once in my life. Hold on, I got a customer. . . ."

He set the phone down, scanned the bag, and said, "Nine fifty-three with tax. Do you need a bag?"

"No bag," Tentacle Guy said. "Thank you."

*Okay,* Buffy thought. *Monsters with manners, too.* Maybe they weren't bad. Just big, scary looking, and misunderstood . . . like Shrek or something.

Tentacle Guy slapped three goo-encrusted coins on the counter. The coins were charred black with gold and crimson specks, and they had small holes in them.

"Keep change," Tentacle Guy said.

"Gah—yuck!" Carrot-top said as his fingers touched the coins.

Buffy silently seconded that. These guys always slimed things, sometimes just to show off that they *could*.

*Don't look up, Carrot-top,* Buffy thought. *Don't look up.*

He didn't. Instead, Carrot-top wiped the coins off with the tail of his red-checked shirt and examined them. "What is this, like Canadian or something? My boss always gets on me when I take Canadian coins. Sorry, got anything else?"

"But this currency bears the sacred blessing of Yiknakt," Tentacle Guy said, sounding a little testy. "It is more than sufficient at the current exchange rate. And the blessing it bears will bring you good fortune."

"Tic Tacs always help, whatever. I don't care if—"

"Yiknakt, the supreme one who sent us on our sacred journey," Tentacle Guy said. His coat was fluttering now. The kitten stuck her head out, said, "Meep!" and leaped to the floor.

"Right on, dude, like I said, Tic Tacs rule, but I still can't take Canadian coinage, sorry."

*"Yiknakt!* Not . . ." Trembling in rage, Tentacle Guy threw back the folds of his dark leather coat, exposing a yawning mouth filled with jagged teeth where his stomach should have been, and streaming tentacles. A horrible stench rose in the air as the mouth opened even wider. "I will feast on the flesh of the unbeliever!"

The other guys in the trench-coat brigade slithered forward. "Don't do it, Fred!"

"Not in front of the kitty!"

Buffy shoved a ten spot across the counter. "Look, guys, the Taste of Sunnydale Sidewalk Fest doesn't start for two weeks, so this one's on me."

Tentacle Guy looked at her. His eyes were wide black saucers stuffed in a face that looked like a bubbling all-meat pizza with all the toppings and some writhing celophods for good measure.

"You propose an exchange?" Tentacle Guy said. "My currency for yours?"

"Hey, I'm all for this Yiknakt guy," Buffy said. "Sounds like an okay guy to me. Yay, Yiknakt, go team go!"

"Are you mocking me?"

"Honestly? Yes. But not Yiknakt. I could use some good luck."

Tentacle Guy turned to his pals. They were anxiously nodding, flapping their tentacles, *go on, Fred, take the exchange!*

Buffy was ready in case he didn't. Her short leather jacket was unzipped, the better to give her access to the handheld double-ax tucked into the back of her waistband. She held her hands behind her, ready to grab and free the ax, her shoulders swaying innocently, eyes wide . . .

She watched Tentacle Guy, his pals, the kitten, the near comatose Carrot-top, who *still* hadn't looked up, and the teenage girl who was flattened up against the freezer door, staring this way in shock.

Buffy noticed the video cameras again.

*Have to come back and do something about those tapes later.*

She wanted to nod toward the teenage girl to try to make it out the back, but she was worried about making any sudden movements.

Tentacle Guy wasn't so worried. He snatched the coins from Carrot-top and slapped them back onto the counter, leaving fresh slime on them. Then he shoved Buffy's ten toward the disrespectful register guy.

Buffy wondered absently if this one would last. Convenience store clerks who worked the night shift in Sunnydale seemed to have a life expectancy slightly less than that of a Spinal Tap drummer. Only without the explosion thing.

Sometimes.

There was a ring, the sound of a drawer opening, and soon some change was slapped down. The cat-food bag was shoved toward Tentacle Guy. All without looking up.

"Next?"

Tentacle Guy crouched and picked up his kitten. She purred. He nodded toward Carrot-top, the chasm of his chest only slightly open now, his tentacles curling hungrily. "He still insulted Yiknakt."

"He's a tool," Buffy said. "You really think Yiknakt would want one of his flock wasting his time on someone like that? Besides, think of the kitty. We could be talking long-term emotional scarring. Kitty-cats who witness violence, you know, it has an impact."

"But she already kills small birds and brings me offerings."

"That's diff—"

"Kitty?" Carrot-top's brow furrowed as he cut Buffy off. "You guys brought a pet in here?" He stood up and pointed at a sign in the window. "No pets allowed. Can't you guys—"

Then he saw them. Finally. He screamed, stumbled back, and snatched up a baseball bat from behind the counter.

"Now he thinks to threaten me?" Tentacle Guy hollered. "For this he will be mine!"

Tentacle Guy allowed Pumpkin, his kitten, to hop from his gray-speckled tentacles. The mouth in his chest opened wide, and a cacophony erupted as tentacles above and below the mouth reached out and wriggled toward their prey.

One of the lightning-quick tentacles was close enough to encircle Carrot-top's neck when a shiny silver flash severed it. Tentacle Guy screamed.

Buffy was up on the counter, slime-covered ax in

hand. *"Not food.* Dork, yes, food, no. How many times do I have to tell you guys?"

Tentacle Guy backed away, withdrawing his horribly writhing celophods.

Buffy shifted her gaze to Carrot-top. He made high, short sharp noises as he hyperventilated. He looked like he needed direction.

"You really are a tool, aren't you? *Run . . .*"

Dropping the bat, he nodded happily—and bolted. He was out the rear exit in moments.

*All-rightee,* Buffy thought as she hopped down from the counter. One civilian cleared, no more incoming, just the teenage girl to worry about.

Tentacle Guy sniffed the air. "It is a Slayer!"

His pals shuddered. "A Chosen One!"

"I told you we should have taken the next exit."

Buffy let the ax dangle at her side. She made sure the ichor didn't get on her nice new boots. "Okay, everyone, let's just chill—"

She heard a shrieking and saw that the chopped-off tentacle was wiggling, spitting, and screaming on its own. Wonderful.

Buffy pointed. "See that thing behind you? Newfangled invention. They call it a door. You open it, you step through, you're somewhere else. No need to say it, I know. Radical. *Crazy.* Would anyone really use such a thing? I don't know. But there it is. Anyway, don't let it hit you on the butt—or whatever—on the way out."

All four trench-coat-wearing monsters clustered by the door, keeping their wide black eyes on the Slayer.

Buffy shook her head. "You see, you're *closer* to *it*— the door, that is—than you are to *me*. Walk away. No one else has to get hurt."

"She will hunt us," Tentacle Guy said, trembling with rage. "Find us wherever we go. And slay us."

Buffy had to admit it. She was perturbed. "What's with the hunting stuff? Just 'cause I'm out every night patrolling, stalking, looking for . . . okay, right. Hunting. Look, I don't suppose this Yiknakt quest ends with my world being threatened, or mass chaos, dogs and cats living together, anything apocalyptic like that?"

"The sacred one is being held hostage. To secure his freedom, we must complete the Babe Ruth baseball card collection of his sworn enemy, Flay the Most Ghastly."

"We are in the blessed minivan, on a quest with many of his greatest cards to trade at the great festival of cards and games in San Diego!"

"Well, there you go!" Buffy said. "What you're up to is no big. No need for slayage on my part. Just, maybe, trade in a few of those cards for local currency. Make transactions easier."

"A good idea," Tentacle Guy said thoughtfully. One of his tentacles reached toward his kitten, who was chasing a small bug across the floor.

"Just collect up the putty-tat and mosey on. Get along now, go, go, shoo, scat!"

The monsters didn't move. Buffy checked the position of the remaining civilian. The girl hadn't taken off, either. It was a real brain trust in here tonight.

*Harsh, harsh, harsh,* she told herself. *How did you react when you were her age and you saw your first monster?*

Buffy raised the ax and sighed. "You're not making with the moseying. Um—now that I think about it—what exactly *will* Yiknakt do once he's free?"

"Set fire to a thousand worlds so that his anger can be seen across the multiverse!"

Buffy sighed and eased herself into a fighting stance. "I don't suppose you could talk him into just having a really big hissy fit?"

"She seeks to lure us into a false sense of security, then attack!" Tentacle Guy hollered as he raced toward Buffy.

His friends joined the assault. "For the honor of Yiknakt!"

"Yes, for Yiknakt!"

Then they were on her. The group attacked as one, attempting to surround her, close off any avenue of escape. Burying her ax in the space between shoulder and neck of the closest monster, Buffy used the momentum of the forward two-handed swing and the purchase her ax had gained to flip herself up and over her attackers. She hauled the ax free as the soles of her boots brushed the ceiling and angled her swiftly descending form so she'd land in the relative safety of the next aisle over. She touched down gracefully, weapon dripping ichor.

*Have to watch for slippery spots,* she cautioned herself.

Buffy was about to check the curved mirrors for the positions of her attackers when a bellow of rage and a sudden explosion of canned goods told her all she needed to know. The lithe Slayer flattened, narrowly escaping some heavy soup cans. She rolled from her belly to her side, quickly taking in the gaping hole that had been a wall of shelves and products separating her from her attackers. A mass of tentacles sprang at her from the gap as she completed her motion, got on her back, and vaulted upward. As her feet hit the ground and she found her center of gravity, Buffy transferred the ax to her left hand and carved a wide swatch through the air.

Whooosh! And eight more spitting tentacles were severed.

Too bad about that ninth one. It whipped around her ankle, the tip separating into five smaller but very strong snakelike "fingers," and yanked her from her feet. She landed hard, her head smacking a half-gallon can of tomato soup, and her grip loosened on the ax just enough that it slipped from her fingers as the tentacle hauled her through the gap.

Buffy saw a cavern lined with sharp, bladelike teeth looming ahead and reached for something—anything— she could use as a weapon.

Heavy soup cans were in both of her hands as she was dragged lightning quick through the opening and toward the hungry mouth in one of the monster's stomachs. She threw both cans at the hole, smashing teeth and causing the monster who'd snatched her to lose his hold and stumble back, the jaws in his belly closed on the leaking soup cans. He looked like he was choking, or needed the Heimlich or something.

Two more squidheads advanced on her from either side of their choking friend, whipping their tentacles around Buffy's arms and hauling her to her feet. Only—she didn't oblige by getting to her feet. Instead, she kicked out, nailing each of the squids clean in the skulls with the heels of her boots. They staggered back, releasing their holds, and Buffy turned and dove through the hole, into the aisle where her ax waited. She tucked and rolled, springing to her feet, almost skidding on a slippery spot.

Her ax was there.

Tentacle Guy had it.

Buffy sidestepped the angry sweep of the blade and performed a backflip and triple somersault to give herself some fighting space. There wasn't much space, though, not in this cramped battlefield. A wall of magazines was at her back, a newspaper stand two feet to her right, then front doors right after that. Tentacle Guy was hollering something that sounded obscene but was probably a prayer in his native language as he barreled headlong at her, ax raised.

*Okay, let's take this outside,* she thought. But a stolen glance at the curved mirror above told her that wasn't going to happen. The other three tentacle dudes were no longer gathered near the register. Instead, they were surging toward the straw-haired girl near the freezer doors.

*Why didn't she clear out? Damn!*

Buffy heard a *meow* and saw the cat now in the gangly girl's arms.

Tentacle Guy, the original, the one and only, was four feet from her, now making a *scrooeeeooouuugh* that sounded like that Waterboy about to attack, when Buffy leaped high and to her left. He swept past her and smashed into the magazine racks as she felt her head smack one of the cork panels of the ceiling and saw the top of some shelving come into view. Buffy kicked away the array of neatly arranged first-aid items with one foot and landed on the other. Keeping her head low to keep from smacking the ceiling lights, Buffy took in the clutter of the long rectangular island ahead. Running fast, she aimed her feet at spaces between boxes of cookies, canisters of peanuts, and sixty-four ounce bottles of Coke and Pepsi.

"Drop the cat!" Buffy yelled, closing on the girl.

"Trying!" the teenager shot back. But now Buffy could see the problem. The cat's claws were hooked on the girl's sweatshirt. The teen was trying to pull the kitten loose, but the screeching animal wasn't cooperating.

A roar came from behind Buffy. Tentacle Guy was after her again. And his buds were closing on the teenager.

Sailing forward atop the aisle, Buffy drop-kicked a heavy bottle of kitchen cleaner at the head of the squid closest to the girl. He grunted and spun around on impact, tripping up the monster behind him.

Buffy was only a few paces away now, but still not close enough. The last member of the trio racing for the teenager was almost on her.

"Give back the sacred pretty-pretty, infidel!" he roared, the tips of his tentacles curling and hardening into razor-sharp claws.

With a grunt, Buffy kicked a six-pack of ginger ale at the monster's head. It missed—and smashed the glass door next to the teen's head. The girl screamed, and the kitten tore free of her. The squid was right on top of her, tentacles slashing downward. Then—

The teenager screamed as the first of the tentacles ripped across her arm. She thrust her hands before her, as if to *shove* the towering squid guy away. Instead, a shrill cry came from the monster, nearly drowning out the sickening *thwock* of something bursting straight through its chest and making the back of its long leather coat suddenly jut out unnaturally.

No, two somethings.

Buffy might have thought the thing had wings. She'd seen that before. But she had a clear view of what had actually happened.

The gangly girl had shoved her hands *right through* the squid's chest.

Buffy had kicked these guys there. She knew how tough and strong that part of their bodies were. No teenager with normal strength could do that. Yeah, there was all that kind of stuff about people lifting cars in moments of distress, but that wasn't what was going on. Buffy couldn't explain why she knew it wasn't that. She just knew. She could feel it.

For a single second, as Buffy leaped toward the girl and the monster, Buffy's gaze locked with that of the teenager, and she *knew* that somehow, they were alike.

Then it was all happening again. In its wild death

throes, the monster's tentacles were coiling, ready to strike, a moment away from tearing the teenager's head from her body. Buffy came crashing down at an angle, putting all her weight on one leg as she wrapped her arm around the monster's neck, hauled it back and away from the teenager—and again, a horrible sound, the ugly, wet, sickening *slorrrp* of the teen's hands and arms sliding free of the dark, spurting, gaping wounds she had created in the monster's chest and her scream, her high, piercing scream of disbelief, of a mind on the verge of shutting down as inhuman blood splashed over her and sprayed across the fractured glass at her back— and spun the monster around to face the onslaught of Tentacle Guy and his stolen ax. The weapon came down and buried itself in the monster's head.

Tentacle Guy released it at once and jumped back in horror and surprise.

"Phil, no!" Tentacle Guy hollered.

Below, the kitten hissed, startling Tentacle Guy for a second.

"Pumpkin?"

And when he looked back, his friend's body was falling, the ax no longer buried in it. There was a flash of silver catching the glare of cheap fluorescent lighting, and behind it, a sweep of blond human hair and a grim face with sternly set features—then everything went cold, and darkness descended.

Buffy stood in front of the terrified teenager. The other two squids raced her way, screaming incoherently. Buffy pivoted, delivering a hard side kick to the chest of the closest squid, slamming him against the glass door with a sharp *crack,* and swung the ax in a wide arc, cutting off his companion's head. She planted both feet firmly as the last squid came at her, tentacles writhing, bad breath bursting from its gaping dagger-lined mouth. She loosed the ax with an overhead tomahawk throw and heard it connect with a dull *thwop*. The beast staggered back, and Buffy closed in, easily avoiding its flying tentacles. She grabbed its coat, spun it around, and brought her knee up to the base of what she hoped would be its spine. There was a loud crackling, and the monster fell, motionless, to the floor. Buffy crouched over it, yanking the ax free, and turned to face the teenager.

The girl was still staring at the squid she had run through, and her own ichor-covered hands.

"It's okay," Buffy said softly. "It's all right, it's over now."

Looking her way with frightened gray-green eyes, the teen gazed at Buffy's face, then down at the weapon the Slayer was still carrying. Buffy flashed an awkward smile and slipped the weapon behind her back. Oops. Not the most nonthreatening way to approach someone.

The kitty-cat was swerving around the remains of its former owner. With an aloof air, the kitten sauntered away toward the rear exit Carrot-top had taken.

"Sorry about all that," Buffy said. "There was supposed to be this part where I held off the bad guys and you ran like hell."

The girl didn't move. She just stood there. Staring.

"I would have been like, *now*," Buffy continued. "Shoo. Shoo! Mush. Scat. Whatever."

The kid was a statue. Her eyes were wide, fixed on the corpse.

"Or—you could have done that all on your own," Buffy suggested, inching closer to the girl and resting the ax on a shelf beside some ichor-splattered bags of chips. "You know, been a self-starter, said, hey, danger over there, safe here, look, an exit. You didn't do that."

"No," the girl said absently.

"You did *that*, instead," Buffy said as she nodded at

the body. "My question, just a little one, don't take me wrong, I'm glad you're not hurt, just—how'd you do that?"

The girl bolted. She sped down the aisle closest to the wall.

Buffy leaped over the pile of squid bodies and raced along the center aisle to cut her off. "Hey, wait!"

Midway down the center aisle, Buffy saw a slick spot. Dark, slippery monster blood and goo. She leaped over it—and a glass jar leaped into the air from the far left lane. It smashed on the floor, spilling pickles and greenish yellow liquid everywhere just as Buffy's feet hit the now slick and slippery floor.

"Whoa!" Buffy hollered. Without an ounce of the grace she had displayed in the battle, Buffy slipped and fell, landing hard on her back. Ahead, she caught a blur of motion as the gangly teen in the dark sweatshirt and jeans ran past the magazines at the end of the aisle. Little bells sounded as Buffy got up and carefully made her way to the front exit, where the glass door was now swinging shut.

The teenager ran across the street, narrowly avoiding an oncoming car, and headed into the park. Buffy chased after her. In seconds they were past the playground, across a clearing, and into the woods.

"I just want to talk to you!" Buffy yelled. "I can help! I'm a friend!"

The girl rabbited into the darkness. Buffy chased her through twisting lanes carved between heavy trees. Twice she caught sight of the girl's blond straggly hair. She tried going around clusters of trees, pushing the girl into traps where she had chased monsters, making new paths, doing everything she could think to catch up with the girl and cut off her flight.

She couldn't.

Finally, Buffy scrambled up into the upper reaches of a towering tree to get a higher vantage. Maybe if she saw where the girl was heading. . . .

She saw nothing. It was as if the girl had disappeared.

Buffy was thunderstruck. Her shoulders sagged. She just wanted to help.

Climbing down to the hard earth, Buffy searched a little longer, then went back to the convenience store to begin her clean up on aisle *everywhere*. The video tape would have to be wiped, the bodies hauled out and buried, those weird coins collected for Giles to study. Plus, she'd have to do it in the dark, with the door locked, to keep anyone from wandering in and getting an eyeful. Hopefully that wouldn't look suspicious to the police.

Yet all those thoughts were background noise for the Slayer as she entered the convenience store and got to work. Her conscious mind was puzzling out the mystery of the strange girl with super-strength: *how* she had managed to get away, and why she was so important.

Buffy felt lost with the girl gone. Like a part of her she'd almost forgotten had briefly shown itself then seen who and what she was now—and ran like hell.

She couldn't leave things like this.

She *couldn't*.

Buffy took care of the mess without incident, stopping only when she came to the collection of items the girl had dropped during the attack. Among them was a paperback novel, a fantasy adventure with a strong female warrior in armor wielding a sword against a misshapen, monstrous giant while villagers cowered behind the fighter or cheered her on. Now *that* seemed like the life, a little public recognition and thanks for doing well at a risky job. The closest Buffy had gotten was her little umbrella at Sunnydale High School on Prom Night.

Sighing, she went patrolling the rest of the night.

It wasn't until an hour later that she remembered the milk and cereal.

Hmmpph. All that and she hadn't even gotten her Twinkie.

# Chapter Two

Arianna DuPrey couldn't stop shaking. She stood outside the door to the cramped two-bedroom apartment she shared with Mother, covered in sweat, dirt, and something black and foul smelling.

Blood.

But not human blood. The things she had seen tonight were not human. The thing she had . . . *killed* . . . it hadn't been human, either.

She looked down in the dim, flickering, amber light of the graffiti-strewn hallway at the tears in her dark sweatshirt. It was so hard to think. If she had been thinking, she would have stripped off the sweatshirt and tossed it into one of the Dumpsters she had passed getting home. Or she would have burned it.

Then it occurred to her—there was *still time*. She could strip it off now, go to the basement, and toss it in the incinerator.

She'd have to explain what happened to it, sure, but

that would be better than the alternative; she didn't *know* what she might face on the other side of that door. What if she walked in and Mother was up waiting for her? If Mother saw her like this—

Arianna put her hands to her head. It was so hard to think. It was like a part of her she had never known existed suddenly woke tonight, and all the rest of her didn't know how to handle it, or what its role would now be in her life. Like she was another person, or had another life, but she knew that wasn't true.

She could barely remember getting home. Or the strange, frightening young woman at the Quick Stop who said she wanted to help. No one could help her. And those who said that they wanted to be her friend always changed their minds soon after. Or never meant it in the first place. . . .

That's right, that's right, she had gone to sleep, then woken up, realizing they were running low on stuff for the morning and she had forgotten to stop at the supermarket on her way home from the library that night. That's why she had gone out so late.

But she had forgotten the milk, the macaroons, the pound cake. She had forgotten it all. There had been screaming and monsters and blood, and it had all gone out of her head, all the important things.

Mother would be furious. It would be horrible. In the morning, so horrible.

And now—

She heard movements in the hall. Someone was coming up the stairs. Was it Mrs. Pasco or Lonnie from next door, Lonnie whose hand-me-downs she wore because they had so little money? It could be someone who'd tell Mother she had been out when she wasn't supposed to be. Someone who would see her like this, shaking, covered in blood and filth. . . . How could she explain? She didn't understand any of it herself.

Hands trembling, Arianna frantically fumbled with her keys. She unlocked the door, slipped into the darkened apartment, and had the door shut behind her before the last footfall sounded from the stairwell.

She was inside now.

Safe. Home—

Arianna gasped and felt her heart leap into her throat as she took in the sight of Mother sitting in her chair with the lights off, waiting, staring, about to rise, about to—

No. It was just Mother's sweater. Arianna scanned the room, praying she was the only one up at this hour. The throw rug on the couch was neatly pinned in place. The apartment's corners were spotless, the floor runners clean. Dishes, plates, glasses, and utensils were all neatly laid out on the dining room table in preparation for breakfast, exactly as she had left them. The *TV Guide* was next to Mother's chair. Everything was as it should be.

At the end of the long corridor was a closed door. Mother's room.

She thought of Mother seeing her like this. What the woman might say or do. What she had faced at the Quick Stop had been scary, but now, this moment, what lay behind that door, was infinitely more terrifying to her. Arianna *had* to get to her room—but her legs wouldn't move. Her body had turned to stone.

Slowly, with more effort, more strength, more *concentration* than she ever felt herself capable of, Arianna dragged one foot forward, then the other. Once she was in motion she moved quickly, quietly—she had learned to be quick, learned to be quiet—and sped down the narrow white corridor, and slipped into her room. She quietly closed the door behind herself but did not lock it. Mother *hated* when she did that. It had only happened once, but the price she'd paid for the affront, for presuming that she was free to lock her door against her mother, to hide anything from her in any place except the confines of her mind . . .

She undressed quickly.

Pale blue moonlight filtered into her room through her curtains. She had one window. It was very small, but without it, she was certain she would have gone mad many, many years ago. She knew that her room was nothing like a typical teenager's room. There were no posters on the walls. Her few belongings were neatly arranged. Her bed was perfectly made.

Suddenly, Arianna heard movement from the hall. She leaped into bed, with her ruined clothing, hauling the blankets up to her neck. Her door opened a crack, and a light swept across her austere room like a searchlight fixed above prison walls. Nasty words were uttered in a low, angry voice. Then the door closed.

Pretending to be asleep, Arianna waited for ten long minutes to make sure her mother hadn't stepped inside and closed the door behind herself in order to trick her. It had happened before.

Finally, she opened her eyes and saw she was alone. Sitting up, Arianna looked at her sweatshirt, then down at her sheets, which were now filthy, too.

The rips could be mended. Everything could be washed and cleaned by morning. She would have to run the water very low so the noise wouldn't be heard by Mother, and it would take almost all night, but it was worth it.

Shuddering, she got up and found a needle and thread. She was an excellent seamstress. She did everything in the house. The cooking, cleaning, mending, laundry, shopping, bill paying. But that was all right. Her mother worked hard. She expected a lot from Arianna, and she had every right to do so.

And she had no problem letting Arianna know when she'd been a disappointment. Which was all the time.

Well, most of the time. There were days when Mother would smile slightly. Days when she had nothing terrible to say. Arianna *lived* for those days.

She looked at the blood around the ripped arm of her sweatshirt. That . . . thing. It hadn't been human. But it had been alive and she had killed it. Did that make her a murderer?

For a short time she had been *out there.* Alone. Alive. *Free.*

She had paid the price for it, too.

Wait—this blood *wasn't* black. It was red. Human blood. She examined her arm in the moonlight. There was a wound, a gash. Why hadn't she felt it?

As she watched, the wound closed and slowly faded away.

*No,* she thought, terrified and confused. She wanted this night to be forgotten, she wanted to dispose of the evidence and never think of it again. But what she had just seen was impossible, what she had done was impossible. And now she was certain she would never forget.

She wished she had one of her books with her, one of her novels of fantasy and high adventure, with women warriors who were brave and true, dragon-riders and monster fighters, an inspiration, an escape from harsh reality. Only—wasn't that what she had witnessed tonight? A true woman warrior, fighting the forces of darkness, with Arianna helping, just a little?

How could all of that be real?

She shook her head. Even if her stories could provide some comfort, help to make order out of the chaos that was her thoughts, she couldn't keep such books here. What if Mother found one? No, they had to be hidden in her locker at school.

Arianna trembled. What was happening to her? What in heaven's name was she becoming? How could she make it stop?

In the darkness, she wept, struggling not to make a sound.

*Help me,* she thought. *Please, someone help me . . .*

Marquis Aurek Kiritan stumbled, clutching at his skull—and was stunned to find the hands of a commoner on him. The short, fat, blue and black skinned vassal helped the towering dark lord to a bench in the dimly lit taproom.

Under any other circumstances, Aurek would have considered the affront of having such scum lay hands on him for any reason a crime punishable by execution, or, at the very least, the loss of a limb or two. But, as the pain subsided and Aurek's head cleared, he found himself in an unusually happy and forgiving mood.

What he wanted most in life was finally in his grasp: *Freedom.*

Aurek looked at the tattered rags the commoner wore. Then he looked down at his own ill-kept leathers. Although they bore the crest of the Monarchy of the Seven Realms, he was the lord of only a pitiful stretch of borderlands.

Perhaps now that would change. . . .

"Marquis, are you well?" the commoner asked. His eyes were bright and yellow. His teeth filed to points. His fingers were wide and crude, the same as his features, not streamlined and smooth, not aquiline like those of a Kiritan. The streaks of midnight blue and faded gold racing through the cracks of his charcoal-colored flesh grew dark, and his pale crimson eyes did not blink.

He should send the man away. He knew it. But an urge came over him. He never talked to filth like this. It was beneath him, even here. Yet that was exactly what he wanted to do. Just until his head cleared. Just to make sure he was thinking clearly, that the excitement over the connection he had felt and all the knowledge it had delivered to his brain hadn't left him addled.

"How well do you know me, Squalor?" Aurek asked. The man's name wasn't really Squalor, so far as Aurek knew. But that was the name he used for everyone in this Godforsaken tract of land. And he could have cared less about their given names.

The slug still didn't know how to answer. "You are the twin moons, the only light, the one true lord of all that is dark and baleful—"

"Stop that or I'll have you killed."

Squalor shut it.

Aurek shifted uncomfortably on the hard wood bench. "I mean, what do you really know of me? Or, I should say, what do you people *think* you know of my past?"

"I wouldn't presume, lord."

"But I'm sure you do, and at every turn, you and all the gossiping vermin like you, so if you want to keep your neck from being broken at this very table, you'll tell me honestly and fully."

So Squalor did. Aurek listened, half-amused, half-enraged. He heard a skewed version of his past. His ambitious younger days, his defiance of authority, the price he had paid.

He drummed his long fingers on the table as Squalor explained that the position Aurek held was one he was forced to assume so that he did not lose his stipend from the true royal family, to whom he was nothing but a very poor relation. His primary duties were to stay away from the Grand Palace and bring no further embarrassment to the Kiritan name.

Much of what Squalor said was true. In his youth he had traveled far from the realms, even to one of the newly discovered dimensions filled with pale "humans." Now he was trapped in this dimension, with no prospects, no hope for advancement. Or so it seemed until a few moments ago.

"You know a thing or two about *want,* don't you?" Aurek muttered. He wasn't entirely certain if he was talking to his vassal or to himself. Or if it mattered. "You know what it means to covet a thing you see but cannot have. You know the bitterness that arises in one's heart when a want is denied. And I'll wager you know the fury that grows from that bitterness."

"I do, sire," Squalor said. "Indeed, I do."

Aurek stared at his hands. They were rough when they should have been smooth. Worn when they should have been fresh. Each day he performed menial tasks that should have been the responsibility of servants. He cooked for himself. Cleaned. Kept his own ledgers. Tended his pathetic garden and effected repairs to his "manor."

His life was pitiful. A joke.

Oh, he was the envy of all around him. His title, his name, his position, his blood heritage. But—what was it he once heard? Judge a man by the company he keeps?

Aurek looked at Squalor. If he was judged now, he would not be found wanting. No, it would be worse than that. He would be found desperate or unclean. Worse, unworthy.

"I'm going to tell you a secret," Aurek said. "One I would share with no other in this realm. Would you like to hear it?"

Even without his enhanced power of intuition—a gift shared by all in his bloodline—Aurek could sense his companion's alarm.

"My lord, mercy," Squalor said. "I suffer from a disorganized mind. My friends tell me that it is my very lack of clarity that keeps me from ever attaining—"

"You have friends?"

"I like to think of them as such. You see, such delicate matters as etiquette and protocol are far beyond me. As such, I've probably made errors during my many years. I *can* learn, if you but teach me, and—"

"This is no trap," Aurek said. "I couldn't care less what you want in life or what wretched things you've done or may yet do to get those things. My observations are about myself. My lot."

Squalor hesitated a moment, then said, "Tell me."

"For a moment, I had been somewhere else. I had been *someone* else."

"Milord?"

"Each member of my bloodline possesses the power to call out to their sire in a moment of deepest need—no matter where either might be. I've felt such psychic 'sendings' before from any of a number of my sons. They were all easy enough to ignore. Not one possessed the strength to send me reeling and clutching at my skull and screaming in agony. Power like what I just felt has not existed among my kind in almost a century. Do you know the power of which I speak?"

"The Reaver," Squalor said softly.

"Yes. It has been nearly a hundred years since a Kiritan was blessed with the power of the Reaver. All have hoped and prayed that a female child would be born to Kiritan blood because the Reaver is always a girl, but in all these years, there have been only sons. Until now. *I* have a daughter, one I never knew existed until moments ago. I'm going to do something now. Guard over my body."

"With my life," the vassal said.

Aurek was certain it was true. He sensed ambition in this man, if not intelligence. Ambition and greed.

Closing his eyes, he whispered an arcane phrase and

felt his spirit lift from his body and travel the pathways beyond the physical. He couldn't describe what he experienced; it would have been like attempting to tell a blind man what purple looked like. No, to describe what purple *tasted* like. Because in this place, the senses were confused, and reason didn't enter into it. He was in a vortex of light and sound, emotion and intellect, memory and foretellings of the future.

He was in the Vast.

Suddenly, he broke through. He found himself sitting in a small, dark room. He found a mirror and gazed into its depths to see an unattractive human girl.

This is where the cry for help had come from.

This was his child.

Retreating immediately, he lavished in the surprise that his daughter lived in the human world he visited close to seventeen years ago. He recalled the woman with whom he had a dalliance and understood now that he left her with a child.

In the taproom, he opened his eyes. "I've found her. I know where she is. I know how to get to her."

Squalor licked his lips in anticipation. "Then you must find her. For the sake of the Seven Realms."

"Accompany me," Aurek said. Rising, he left the inn without a backward glance. He had very little time to prepare for the journey before him, very little time to find his little girl and do what must be done. He was certain that if he succeeded in his quest, he would become one of the most powerful creatures in any of the Seven Realms— or in the worlds beyond.

Outside, Squalor spread his arms to the dark sky. "The Seven Realms, they will be ours!" Squalor cried. "And then, all that lies beyond. With the power of the Reaver at our command, we will be unstoppable!"

*We?* Aurek thought. *Ah . . . no.*

"What is your real name, anyway?" Aurek asked mildly.

"Pie, milord. Short for Pieopholus Duruch Mensopheas of the—"

The toady didn't finish. Aurek was on him so swiftly, he didn't even know what was happening. All he saw was a blur—then darkness.

Aurek stood over the minion whose neck he had just snapped in the alleyway. "You presumed too much, Squalor. Just because I felt a need to talk and promised not to snap your neck at the table did not mean I needed a partner."

Aurek sighed. If only he had a servant, a true, trusted confidante. Or, better, a bitter slave, like Aurek himself. The amusement of waiting for the slave to rebel, or attempt rebellion, the unspoken promise of death between them, the torture and the pain. . . .

He shuddered. The thought of inflicting such misery was absolutely *scrumptious*.

But it would have to be someone with brains enough to know when to keep quiet. Someone of a better class than pitiful Squalor here. Maybe someone he would find along the way. He had a rather long journey ahead of him, in any case. A journey that would end in *freedom*.

Gazing at the black suns and the eternal twilight of the borderlands' sky, Aurek allowed his dark heart to fill with hope for the future.

# Chapter Three

**D**awn Summers drew a deep breath, psyching herself up for the conflict ahead. Her sister, sitting beside her in the swelter of their mom's parked car, looked equally ill at ease.

The off-white walls of the squat building ahead drew the life from the sun, absorbing its last amber rays and turning them to shadow. Its square eyes shimmered gleefully with crimson streaks it stole from the darkening sky.

School always sucked. This one sucked everything dry. People, places, things. Didn't matter. Sunnydale Schools had an unquenchable appetite. A lust for life. It reveled in crushing the backbone of its prey and draining them of every last bit of vitality. It delighted in the dying of the light.

Tonight, its doors were propped open, and a steady flow of prey entered its greedy mouth. Well-dressed men and women herded their children before them, noting the hesitation of the young who were exchanging patient, smiling, knowing glances.

Only a few students entered the school for Parent-Teacher's Night with perfect chins raised and beautiful eyes set dead ahead: the predators. These had nothing to fear. The school respected them; it loved, sheltered, and cultivated them. They were stunning, they were pristine, they radiated false or stolen light, and they hid their darkness well. But, behind perfect clothes and perfect smiles and perfect grades, they were evil.

*Too bad slaying doesn't run in the family. . . .*

Buffy and Dawn pulled down the driver and passenger-side vanity mirrors on the back of the sun visors. The air-conditioning had quit on the drive over, leaving them with windblown hair to fix and makeup to retouch.

"How ya doin?" Buffy asked.

Dawn shrugged. "Fine. Why wouldn't I be?"

Buffy tossed her hair over one shoulder. "You tell me. You're the one acting all jittery."

"I am *not*. You're the one who's wigged."

"Not a bit."

Dawn put away her lip gloss. "Fine."

"Fine."

They both hesitated before getting out. The car felt like Joyce Summers. Smelled like her. Brought back memories.

Each of the young Summers women often made excuses not to get into the car, but once they did, neither ever wanted to leave. It was comfort. It was love.

Yet, one day, it, too, would no longer be in their lives.

They approached the doorway. Dawn tensed up. They were going in.

Right into the belly of the beast.

Buffy put her hand on Dawn's shoulder. Dawn wasn't sure if the gesture was meant to be reassuring or if her older sister was *looking* for comfort. Either way, it wasn't happening. The harsh glare of overhead lighting glimmered off trophy cases and framed watercolors from art class. Tacky little signs were taped to the prisonlike cinderblock walls welcoming parents and identifying "Ms. Green's Biology" and "Mr. Ellsworth's History." To Dawn, it felt like a game of Clue. *Ms. Green did it in the biology room with the—*

She would have said they still needed the weapons, but the weapons were there: cutting words. Stabbing glances. Sharp wits.

A murmur, a buzz, slowly rising, reached Dawn's ears. Parents, teachers, and students broke into little clusters—small, cancerous growths breaking off from the mother mass and looking to grow into full-fledged health risks in the hall, hiding their true natures with deceptively bright-colored dresses and business suits and false white smiles. Several groups drifted toward the auditorium, where refreshments would be served.

Everywhere Dawn looked she saw people happily chatting in their own little circles, their own little worlds. Around them, the soft gray and blue of the walls pressed closer, and the *click-clack-click* of busily approaching high heels rose and fell as people bustled past the duo. Dawn did her best not to choke on the overwhelming smell of too much "manly" cologne in the air from all the dispirited dads who hid their desires to be anywhere but here less well than their wives. A few teachers passed, wearing similarly overpowering scents meant to mask Pigpen-like clouds of smoke clinging to hair-helmeted coifs and department store clothing.

It wasn't just the place that was getting to Dawn as Buffy slipped one arm in hers and walked her toward the auditorium. The place was bad enough. It was where she had been told . . .

*About Mom.*

No, there was more. More even than the stylish students, the pretending parents, the trying teachers. Dawn thought about what she'd been doing lately. All of the things she'd been up to. Cutting class. Her grades going to hell. The pranks. The stuff that was missing or busted, all courtesy of her own late-night rendezvous with this hateful place when Buffy was on patrol.

The auditorium was decked out with banners, and there were several tables filled with soft drinks, punch, cookies, cakes, and health food hors d'oeuvres. Colored balloons tied to the tables bobbed like sycophants. At least these bore truer colors. Glistening bloodred. Gleaming forest green. Glowering midnight blue. The colors of anger masquerading as discipline, of the promise of freedom seen and felt but only on a playing field within fenced-in grounds, of wretched pain trying desperately to pass itself off as learning and growth.

And the music . . . Britney, Christina, Backstreet Boys . . . the stuff "grown-ups" couldn't avoid being blasted with when they went to music and video stores, the sounds they thought had to be what "kids" liked. Dawn considered counting how many heads were really moving to the beats and nailing down an average age. But she had more important things on her mind.

Buffy and Dawn stood alone. Mothers and daughters swarmed around them, a few casting sidelong glances at the nervous pair. The way one of the parents looked at her made Dawn suddenly wish *she* had superpowers. Then she could make herself invisible, and no one would be able to give her *that look* of half-pity, half-gratitude, ever again.

*Thanks, kid. See, it's like the lottery. Every year or so, someone's got to lose a parent. Your mom dying like that means the rest of us can relax. No one else's number will be called for a long time.*

Or maybe if she had powers, she would just teleport herself somewhere else. Anywhere else. Anywhere but here.

*Where was Melissa?* Her friend was supposed to be here early, waiting, ready. That was the *plan.*

"So . . . ," Buffy said.

Dawn shrugged and slipped her hands behind her back. It was that or start wringing them. "So."

"You want to show me around? Make with the introductions?"

Dawn's loopy smile, already in place without her even noticing, widened. She wondered how stupid she looked.

"Are you okay?" Buffy asked.

"Fine."

"Something in your teeth? Practicing for a dental floss commercial?"

Dawn laughed way too hard at a throwaway that wasn't even funny. When she recovered, she said, "Fine . . ."

Buffy shook her head and looked away. "So . . . refreshments? Introductions? Explanation of why we're just standing here not mingling?"

"Not feeling mingly," Dawn said.

"Okay, I guess I'll just start flagging people down," Buffy said, raising one hand.

Dawn gasped. Buffy was about to do just that.

"Subject change," Dawn said quickly, snatching her sister's hand. "Concert. Two weeks from Saturday. At the coliseum. Planning on going."

"Unplan," Buffy said. "We didn't discuss this."

"It's not like I'm a little kid or anything," Dawn said. "You trust me, right?"

Buffy frowned. "The coliseum's a two-hour drive. How were you planning on getting there?"

"Hitchhike. Only take rides from scabby-looking old guys with handcuffs on the dash. The usual."

"Funny. Big funny hah-hah. Seriously, this is not—"

"There you are!" a friendly voice called.

Dawn looked up and saw Melissa and her mom coming to the rescue. Melissa looked perfect. Her long brown hair swept just past her shoulders, and her bangs were expertly cut. Her makeup accentuated her pretty mocha skin and subtly complemented her hot pink sweater, denim skirt, and sandals. Her mom wore a stylish pink dress.

They chatted Buffy up fast, got her into friendly mingle-mode, and before Buffy knew what was going on, Melissa's mom had her arm around Buffy and was leading her away.

"Your mom's really okay with this?" Dawn asked.

Melissa grinned. "Running interference? Keeping your sister away from the principal and any nonfriendlies on the teaching staff or parental types? Oh, yeah. She loves it. Makes her feel our age again." She shrugged. "Want some punch?"

"Kinda feeling punchy enough. But maybe. Sure."

Dawn followed her pal across the auditorium. They were halfway to the first snack table when the predators approached, a bounce in their step, all smiles, smirks, and grins. Dawn knew this pack intimately. Kirstie and her friends. Cardigan-wearing rumor mongers, spreaders of lies, and makers of misery.

The Sweater Mafia. In this place, they were *adored*.

"Holding back," Melissa said.

Dawn and Melissa watched Kirstie eye the gathering with a nasty little smile, hunting for prey. Only those with no light, no life, no hope would do. Dawn was sure of it. She'd seen Kirstie like this before, her movements just a little exaggerated, her voice a little too loud, her friends a little more scared and tense than usual. Something must have happened to put her in a bad mood. Maybe it was having to share the spotlight with her mother.

And there—standing on line behind the punch bowl, a little paper plate with cookies and crumb cake in her long-fingered hand—was the prey. Best of all, there were no adults near the refreshments at the moment. It was perfect timing. Kirstie zeroed in on her and raised her cheerleader perfect chin majestically. Her flowing blonde hair shone like an angel's aura.

"I don't want to see this," Dawn said.

"Okay," Melissa agreed.

Kirstie drew closer to her intended, sweeping through the line as if its boundaries meant nothing to her. She moved like a spirit on light blue high-heeled sandals, her light blue dress flowing elegantly with her movements.

Dawn hated her.

"So how come neither of us is moving?" Melissa asked. "Please tell me this isn't slow-down-on-the-highway-to-watch-the-car-wreck syndrome."

It wasn't. But . . . Dawn couldn't quite put into words why she wasn't moving. Why she felt drawn to watch this.

Maybe it was because she wanted to do more than just watch.

*Stop it,* Dawn screamed in her skull. *Go over there and keep it from happening!*

Kirstie was on her prey now. Tugging at the tall, gangly girl's old and out-of-style dress, a hand-me-down dark green Dynasty collection number altered to *kind* of fit. It was short, ending mid-calf when it should have reached to her ankles. The girl's straggly hair was caught up in a Julia Stiles wanna-be pull-back. Her makeup wasn't much, and her shoes didn't really go with her outfit.

Dawn sort of knew her. They had a class together,

though Dawn wasn't sure which one. Maybe art. Dawn's attention was always on Kevin when she was there, so yeah, art, probably. . . .

She didn't know the girl's name, but she had seen people pointing at her and had heard the things they said, like she was poor, her clothes were boy's clothes, mostly, from some neighbor. She didn't have a dad, not that anyone knew about, just a mom who worked a lot.

Ahead, the action got started. . . .

Acting as if she were raising her hand to touch her own hair, Kirstie knocked the little plate from the teen's trembling hands. The girl drew back in surprise, and Kirstie managed to have her leg thrust out in just the right position so the girl would trip over it. She went down hard, smacking all of her weight on the edge of the table. A huge gasp came from the onlookers as the table pitched forward, the rear edge lifting into the air, and the punch bowl slid and went down with the floundering girl whose left shoe heel was breaking as she faltered and fell. The contents of the bowl splashed down on her head, covering her face, hair, and neck with pinkish punch and bits of fruit.

An explosion of laughter rocked the gathering, and the music came to a stop. Suddenly, everyone was watching Kirstie and her victim.

"Omigosh, what *happened?*" Kirstie said, looking down at the mess she'd made as if she were seeing it for the first time. She crouched beside the girl. "Are you okay?"

"Get away from me!" the girl screamed, shoving Kirstie's "helping hands" from her.

"Whoa," Kirstie said as she rose and backed away. "Hey, just trying to help."

The girl stared at the rapidly spreading puddle of pink liquid as if she were going into shock.

Kirstie stepped away from the slippery spot. She muttered, just loud enough for the students nearby to hear, "Some people can't hold their punch, I guess."

The laughter rose again from Kirstie's clutch. Now adults were rushing their way, and the luxury of a malicious smile Kirstie had allowed herself was withdrawn.

"What's going on here?" a stern-faced balding man said as he stormed forward. Mr. Aimes wore a dark JCPenney's bargain suit and a tie with bug-eyed guppies staring out of a fish tank. He was a gym teacher, with a muscular build that made his sleeves look like they might burst from a Hulk-out at any second.

"I was—" the girl started. She closed her eyes. "I just wanted some—"

"She tripped," Kirstie supplied. "It wasn't her fault."

"Yeah, look at those feet," one of the boys said. "Bigfoot ain't got nothin' on those."

"Better not let Sasquatch out of the house," another one added.

More laughter, more insults. Kirstie didn't have to say a thing. She had gotten the momentum started. Now the incident was taking on a life of its own.

"Here," Mr. Aimes said, frowning as he offered his hand to the girl. Then—

he slipped on the slick floor, going right down on his butt, his feet flying high in the air, his tie desperately reaching to defy gravity, then settling.

Then all the other adults were clustered around the teacher, checking his skull, worrying over him.

Kirstie's victim was alone. The music started up, and Kirstie's mom rushed to her side, putting a protective arm around her daughter, looking down at the shell-shocked mess of a teen on the floor with contempt.

Dawn felt Melissa's hand on her arm.

"Come on, let's go," Melissa said.

Shrugging off her friend's arm, Dawn shook her head. "You go."

Melissa sighed. "I'll be around."

Near the table, Kirstie was again without her mom. The adults had helped Mr. Aimes to a chair near the wall and were clustered near him. Someone's dad was a doctor who was checking the teacher out, asking him questions about the year and who was president. . . .

Kirstie's malicious glee wasn't hidden as she looked down at her victim. "All alone, Little Miss Thing? No parent on Parent-Teacher's Night? Wow, that's surprising. What, did your mom just promise she'd be here then not show? I wouldn't have, if I were her. Who needs that kind of embarrassment?"

The girl didn't say anything. She was trying to get to her feet, but her broken shoe heel and the punch slick were making it difficult. Dawn looked around for Buffy, but her sister was nowhere in sight. She was probably off on a classroom tour with Melissa's mom.

None of the guys offered any help. No one did.

This was wrong. Being different, being poor, being raised by a single parent, and being too sensitive and lacking in confidence—none of these things were reasons why anyone should be treated so badly. Dawn knew what it was like to feel different from everyone else.

Suddenly finding her feet in motion, Dawn boldly went where no sane person had gone before.

"Hey, what's the deal?" Kirstie asked as Dawn approached.

Dawn didn't make eye contact. Her shoulders were tight, she knew what she was doing was crazy, but to do nothing like everyone else . . . that was worse.

She crouched near the girl and gathered up the tablecloth lying bunched and partially trapped by the upended table. Without saying a word, she worked it free and spread it out like a towel, letting it soak up the worst of the punch. Then she reached over and touched the girl's ankle, trying to get her fingers on the strap holding the broken shoe in place. The girl tensed and flinched.

Dawn met her gaze. *Just let me help,* Dawn thought. *Just let me.*

The girl looked away, chest heaving. By the time Dawn had the shoe off, no one was looking their way any longer. Kirstie glanced in her direction, her face flush with fury, but all the others simply appeared shamed and no longer able to understand what was funny about any of this in the first place.

"Where's your mom?" Dawn asked.

The girl's hair was undone, some of the strands dangling in her face, pink droplets dripping from their tips. Lemon halves lolled on her shoulders. She didn't look at Dawn. "Working . . . supposed to be here . . . working."

"You want to leave? My sister's here. We could give you a ride."

The girl shook her head, and pink droplets sprayed from her hair. Her busted shoe was off, and she removed the other one on her own, though her hands were shaking.

"Called her from the pay phone," the girl said. "She might show later."

Dawn nodded and put her hand on the girl's shoulder. "How about—I dunno, how about we go to the girls' room, I can help you clean—"

"Get away from me," the girl hissed. She pushed Dawn away, but not hard enough to knock her off balance.

"Okay, fine," Dawn said. She got to her feet and backed off as the girl rose, her shoes in her hand. She looked like she'd just been run over by a catering truck. Soggy pink stained dress. Lemon halves and cookies crumbs and cake wedges plastered to her body.

"Go on, laugh," the girl said. Her features were steely. "It's funny."

"No, it isn't," Dawn said.

"I know this one," the girl whispered. She angled her head in Kirstie's direction. "Bad cop." Then to Dawn. "Good cop. Good cop says, 'I just want to help, I just want to be your friend, then it's, oops, there's Charlie Brown up in the air, Lucy pulled the football away. Hah-hah, everyone has a great time.'"

"No, it's not like that—"

"Yeah, right. Tell me what it's *like.*"

Dawn didn't have to. Kirstie and her flock sauntered by.

Kirstie shrugged. "Yeah, well I think Mrs. Summers croaked because having to deal with a little dweeb like that all the time made something pop in her brain. . . ."

Dawn paled. She felt sick inside. Her fault? They were saying what had happened to her mom was her fault?

Dawn wanted to scream. She wanted to pick something up and throw it. Trembling, she wanted to launch herself at Kirstie and make her take it back!

A hand touched her arm and made her jump. She looked over swiftly, surprised to see the pink-haired, gangly girl's softened expression.

"I'm . . . my name's Arianna."

"Arianna," Dawn repeated. It was pretty. A pretty name. She put her hand on her forehead. "I wanna kill her."

"I know. Believe me, I know."

Dawn's world started blurring. "Oh, no. I'm crying. I am, aren't I? Everything's gonna run . . ."

"Yeah, you'll look worse than me."

Dawn felt the first flickerings of a smile come on her.

"I'm Dawn," she said. "Dawn Summers. . . ."

# Chapter Four

Buffy crossed the park, heading for the Quick Stop where the strange, straggly-haired girl had gotten away from her two nights ago. She would have been searching last night, but that would have meant not being there for Dawn on Parent-Teacher's Night.

She was the Slayer-in-Black this evening. Black sleeveless turtleneck, black bootcut leather pants, black high-heeled boots. It suited her mood.

A wind kicked up, and she hugged herself against the evening chill. Maybe the sleeveless hadn't been the best idea. Ditto on the company.

"Slow down now, eh, luv?" Spike said. His long, leather coat fluttered behind him as he hurried to keep up. Moonlight glistened off his platinum hair.

"What's the matter?" Buffy said with a smirk. "Can't keep up?"

"Oh, I can keep up with *you*, missy. Never you mind. I'm just wondering what the hurry is?"

Spike raced in front of the purposefully striding, serious-faced Slayer.

"This girl's in trouble," Buffy said. "She needs my help."

"Oh, really? So *that's* why she took off like a shot when you tried talking to her last time."

Buffy growled.

"Just going on what you tell me." His arms outstretched, Spike spun like a child in the soft moonlight. Then he took a deep breath of the chilly air and grinned. "Now *that's* just the thing, isn't it?"

Buffy stalked past him. "Anyone ever point out how seriously weird you are?"

"Only you, every chance you get," Spike said. He thrust his hands in his pockets and sped up his pace to keep up with his companion. "It's one of the many signs of your unspoken affection for me."

"Unspoken because it only exists in your head."

"A matter of perceptions," Spike said. He ran to a carousel and leaped on it, whirling in an ever wider circle. "You've got to loosen up, Buffy. Live in the moment. Enjoy yourself."

Buffy ground to a stop. Her lowered head bobbed, as if she were nodding in agreement, or, at least, seriously considering Spike's words. Encouraged, he leaped from the carousel—

And she was on him, grabbing one arm before he hit the ground, whipping him around in a tighter, more painful arc, tossing him to the ground. He grunted as he struck the sodden earth and rolled, then gasped as a Prada boot landed on his rock-hard stomach, pinning him in place, and an all too familiar stake swept down at his heart.

Mr. Pointy stopped a centimeter away from breaking undead skin—though it did pierce the vampire's black shirt.

"Now *that's* going to leave a nasty little hole," Spike said with a laugh. He loved this little game they played. Once, it might not have been anything like this. He had genuinely wanted to kill the Slayer. But a lot had happened since those days. Now his feelings for Buffy were . . . different.

"Who's going to pay for the mending?" Spike asked. "You?"

"It's a T-shirt," Buffy said firmly, clearly intent on puncturing his mood. "T-shirts are cheap. They can be replaced. Not like some other things."

Spike looked away and let out a deep breath. "Are you gonna let me up or are we gonna get lost in this ocean of red-hot sexual tension between us?"

Buffy stepped away, slipping her stake into her jacket. "I should have done you just for that."

"Promises, promises," Spike said as he sat up and dusted himself off. Catlike, he sprang to his feet. The Slayer was already on the move, navigating a small grove of tightly placed trees.

"Done, as in dusted, as in killed, as in *slain,* duh!" Buffy said. "You are so gross."

"Touchy, touchy, aren't we?"

"I just don't know why I let you tag along," Buffy said. She didn't even have to look down to avoid a thick twisted root below her. Spike, on the other hand, had to leap back as she allowed a branch she'd bent out of the way for herself to nearly slap him in the face.

"Oh, is that what I'm doing?" Spike said. "Tagging along? I thought I was here to help. That *is* all I want to do, you know. Help."

Buffy tried to tune Spike out. When she'd gone to the Bronze and found no one to join her but him, Buffy thought a little company might be a good thing. She'd been alone way too much lately, and when she was, she dwelled on things she couldn't do anything about. Things like her mother's death.

A smug look appeared on the vampire's face. "I know why you asked me to come along."

"I *asked* you?"

Spike shrugged. "All your other friends have lives, luv. Don't have that problem with me."

"I could take that on so many levels, but in the great game of life, I roll the dice and all I keep landing on is *yuck*." She shuddered. "And you're *not* my friend. I don't know what you are."

"Handsome and devilishly clever come to mind."

"Again, with the yuck. No, wait, I've got it. Convenient. That's what you are."

"Your flattery warms my heart."

"Ewww. Is that even possible?" Spike raised an eyebrow and was about to speak when Buffy cut him off. "I don't want to know. Anyway, I guess walking along *with* you is better than having you stalking me."

"Wot? Now hold on—stalking? You think I'm—" Spike stepped in front of her as they emerged from the park. The convenience store was across the street. "Bloody hell—look. I *have* stalked. I *will* stalk again. That's a predator's job when seeking prey, and it'll be my job again when I have this bloody inhibitor chip out of my head that soldier boy's surrogate mum put there. Oh, yeah, I *know* a thing or two from stalking, you bet I do. And if I was stalking, *you* wouldn't know it, girlie. Otherwise, it wouldn't *be* stalking, now would it?"

"Except all those times you wanted me to know."

"Protecting! I was protecting! Keeping an eye out. Watching for ultimate evil and whatever. Bloody hell . . ."

Buffy swept beyond him. "Excuse me."

"So, this girl," Spike said as he caught up with her. The streets were dead, yet he noticed that Buffy didn't even look to see if any cars might be coming. Not a good sign. She was either being careless . . . or feeling something worse. "The one you had the run in with the other night. What's up with her again?"

They stopped in front of the Quick Stop. Buffy looked through the window and saw Carrot-top. She was amazed he'd come back to work. Relieved, too. He was her only lead. And she wanted to find that girl. Needed to find her.

"You ever wonder what it would be like?" Buffy asked.

"Might help if I knew the topic of this conversation. . . ."

"The girl. Why I want to find the girl. Do you ever wonder what it would be like if things were different? If you hadn't been turned by Drusilla?"

"I'd be dead, sweetie. Dust by now. It was a long time ago."

Buffy growled. "You're the one who asked."

Pulling his fingers across his lips, Spike made a "zipping it" motion with a bold flourish and closed his mouth tightly.

"This girl is out there. She's alone. She's scared. She doesn't understand what's happening to her. Who only knows how she got her power, who only knows what she might do with it." Buffy stopped herself. This was hard for her to talk about. When she looked into that girl's eyes, all she could see was herself at that age. The way she had been when she had first found out she was different. No one had offered Buffy a choice about what kind of life her powers would give her. Buffy *couldn't* let that happen to this girl. She would have a choice—Buffy would make sure of it.

"We're going to find her," Buffy said. "That's it."

"Right on, it's a plan." Spike stood back as Buffy

hauled the glass door open. "She didn't leave a credit card behind, now did she? Personal check? Maybe she was wearing one of those bracelets. You know, 'Call in case superpowers suddenly spring up,' one of those things?"

Buffy tried to let the door hit Spike in the face, but he was too fast for her.

Oh, well. She'd have other chances.

Dawn peered over the brim of the wide steaming bowl at her nervous guest.

"They were supposed to be cheeseballs," Dawn said. She stood in the kitchen of the Summers home, a nasty burning smell wreathing her. Arianna gulped as she looked down into the bubbling surface of the horror masquerading as a wholesome movie snack.

"I think there's supposed to be more than one," Arianna said.

Dawn grimaced. "I think it must be destroyed."

"Before it replicates?"

"I hadn't even thought of that. I was just worried it might try to get out and eat us."

"How about you dump it out and I'll clean up in here?"

Dawn set the bowl down carefully on the counter. "You're my guest. You should go be doing guestly things. Not cleaning up my messes."

"Really, I don't mind," Arianna said. "I, uh . . . my mom works a lot. I have to cook for myself. Got any popcorn?"

"The nonlethal kind?"

"Little unthreatening bags, microwaves, it's usually pretty safe."

"Yeah," Dawn said as she rummaged through a cupboard. Two entire shelves were empty. All of her mother's favorite foods used to reside there.

Neither she nor Buffy could bring themselves to put anything in those places.

Dawn snatched up some microwavable popcorn and gave it to Arianna. "Here ya go!"

"Great," Arianna said.

Dawn took care of the cheeseball from hell and turned to see Arianna staring at a schedule held to the refrigerator door by a bunny-shaped kitchen magnet. The list divided up who would take care of dinner, laundry, cleaning, cooking, and so on, for the entire week. Dawn did it some of the time, her older sister Buffy the rest.

"This is . . . amazing." Arianna smiled and put on the microwave popcorn.

"If you say so." Dawn checked her dark green sweater and jeans to see if any gunk had gotten on her. Nope. Not a trace of it. Cool. She didn't want to mutate.

Arianna's head was down as she busily soaked the pots Dawn had used to concoct the horror. "And with a good scouring and a blessing from a priest, a rabbi, and a licensed exorcist, I think we can keep these seemingly innocent household items from ever misbehaving and creating such a thing again."

Dawn nodded. "I'm down with that." She smiled. "You're funny, you know that?"

Arianna's went impossibly wide. "You really think so?"

Arianna pulled on her ratty oversized navy blue sweater and sent a frown at her baggy faded blue jeans, and worn sneakers. "Someone says that, I always think they mean funny looking, or funny strange. I hate wearing this stuff. Hand-me-downs, nothing fits right. I'm surprised you're even willing to be seen anywhere with me, the way I dress."

"Never entered my mind. I meant funny in the *best* way, and believe me, funny is a good thing. You don't know how bad I just need to laugh sometimes," Dawn said. "Things get a little tense with my sister sometimes. She just doesn't get it, y'know? It's like she doesn't even remember how it was when she was fifteen. You just need a little freedom sometimes."

"Yeah," Arianna said softly. She eyed the clock. "I, uh, I have to be careful how long I stay out."

*That's a weird way to put it,* Dawn thought. *Careful? Of what?*

The silken-haired Summers girl hopped up onto the counter, snatching the DVDs they had rented. "Okay, so, we've got *Bloodsucking Freaks, Psycho Beach Party,* and *Old Yeller.* My friend Willow—really, she's Buffy's friend, and she's really cool—she said *Old Yeller* was the scariest, but I hear there's this really hot guy in *Psycho Beach Party*—"

"Hot guys," Arianna said as she turned off the water and dried off her hands while the microwave went off. "Can never go wrong with that."

"The motion is seconded and carried," Dawn said. They found a bowl for the popcorn and headed off to the living room.

While Dawn popped in the DVD, Arianna made herself comfortable on the couch. "I don't have any brothers or sisters," Arianna said softly.

"Lucky you," Dawn said. "It was one thing when Mom was here, but now . . ."

"Must be nice, though, having someone to talk to, having someone there."

Dawn relented. "You're right. You've got your mom . . ."

"Right," Arianna said weakly. "So, come on, bring on the hot guys!"

Dawn plopped down on the couch, rocking the big bowl of popcorn in Arianna's lap. She picked up her diet soda and raised it in a toast. Arianna felt swept away by her friend's wide, perfect smile, and the warmth that radiated from the girl. She quickly got her can. They clanked them together, managing not to spill any.

"Here's to one night of freedom," Dawn said.

Arianna looked at the clock again. In a small voice she said, "To freedom."

Arianna and Dawn were having a great time a half hour later when someone opened the front door but did not step through. Raised voices sounded from the front stoop outside. Dawn turned to the window and saw Buffy and Spike arguing.

"All over my favorite coat, thank you," Buffy hollered.

"How was I to know that's what happened when you shake 'em up?" Spike called.

A Miss Piggy–caliber cry of frustration echoed from outside. "Oh, like you haven't played with those before. Look at this. Some stains don't come out, I'll have you know."

"Fine, then! Next time, you figure out a way of getting the attention of the bloody convenience store clerk when he won't get off his soddin' cell phone and answer a few simple, civil questions!"

"My sister," Dawn said, turning to her friend, who looked really uncomfortable. Dawn jacked up the TV's volume. "No big. Welcome to Bizarro World."

"Um . . . I should get going," Arianna said. "There's something I've got to take care of. I can . . . I can come right back. Be like an hour. I'm sorry. A call. My mom. She expects me to be there when she calls from her break. It's . . ."

Dawn was only half-listening. "The phone? Call your mom? Sure, *mi casa loca casa,* but you're welcome to it." She absently dropped the phone next to Arianna.

The tall girl stared at it. "You're right . . . I could just call my mom at work and pretend I'm at home. She wouldn't know the difference."

Suddenly, Dawn heard footsteps. Someone entered the house from the stoop—and stopped dead.

"It's *her*," Buffy said, startled.

Arianna looked up sharply. Dawn was surprised by the shocked expression Buffy and Arianna shared. No, it was more than shock. It was recognition.

But—how could they know each other?

To Dawn's further surprise, Arianna leaped from the couch and hurled the bowl of popcorn at Buffy.

"Whoa!" Buffy called, deflecting it easily—it went right out the door and at Spike.

"Wonderful, wonderful, now I'm going to be picking popcorn out of my hair," Spike muttered.

Dawn heard a crash of breaking glass and turned quickly to see Arianna diving through the shattered window frame across the room. She landed beyond some shrubbery and sprang into a run through the darkness.

From the porch, Spike called, "Want me to track her, then? Think I've got her scent. Me being such an expert at hunting, oh, no, what was the word you used? Right, 'stalking,' that was it. . . ."

Dawn was off the couch, wandering toward the shattered window, trying to make sense of what she'd just seen, when Buffy came up beside her.

"Dawn, I need your help. That girl's in trouble. At least, I think she is. She might be. I need to talk to her."

"Yeah," Dawn said. "You and me both."

# Chapter Five

Arianna raced home and was there when her mother called. She desperately wanted to tell her mother what was happening, to ask for comfort and advice, but she knew that wasn't what she would get. Her mother only barely tolerated her presence now. If she knew Arianna was a freak, there was no telling how she'd react. Not well, Arianna wagered. She was alone in this.

Claiming she was sick, Arianna got off the phone with her mother quickly, then went to her room to think about what had happened and what she would do next.

Dawn's sister hadn't even tried to follow her, and Arianna didn't think that was because of how she'd eluded the young woman the other night. No, Buffy had let her go for some other reason. Arianna had somehow *sensed* as much during their brief second meeting.

Even though she was certain Buffy meant her no harm, Arianna had panicked at the sight of her. *Why?*

*Because she knows what you are. Or, at least, she knows what you can do. And there are things she can do, too. . . .*

Buffy was strong, like Arianna had suddenly become, and the way she acted at the Quick Stop made it clear that the sight of actual monsters wasn't anything new to her. But if Arianna hadn't seen Buffy in action, she never would have known there was anything unusual about her. Maybe that meant Arianna could blend in, too. It may have even been what Buffy wanted to tell her. If she was smart, if she kept a low profile and didn't use her powers unless she really needed to, then it was possible she could have a normal life.

*Yeah, like this is normal. . . .*

And the whole thing with Dawn—looking back on it, she found it hard to believe that Dawn had set her up, that she had known her sister was looking for her, that she had known all along that Arianna was different. Yet she'd reacted the way she'd been taught to react, to think the worst, the absolute worst, of anyone, and to act on that assumption even when her instincts were telling her the truth was something different.

It's just . . . Arianna wanted normalcy. She'd seen Dawn as a way of having just that. A friend who wouldn't see her as strange, who would accept her as any other girl. She didn't know if that was possible now.

She didn't want to be a freak; she hadn't asked for any of this. That was why she didn't even try to fight back when Kirstie went after her during Parent-Teacher's Night. She knew what she had done to that creature at the Quick Stop and that she could have done the same or worse to Kirstie. As much as she hated the girl, Arianna didn't want to be responsible for hurting anyone like that.

*So why did I run?*

She knew. It was because the sight of Buffy made it

real, made it impossible for her to tell herself nothing weird was going on, that she wasn't trapped in some nightmare, that she wasn't becoming a freak.

Shuddering, Arianna got undressed and went to bed long before her mother got home.


Arianna was lost in one of the most vivid and haunting places she had ever visited in dreams. It was peaceful and serene. Magical.

She stood within an ever-changing garden filled with colorful alien flora. The beautiful flowers opened and sang to her. Violet eyes opened and winked at her upon twisting, shimmering, rainbow-colored vines. Leaves floated from the ground to the sky, dancing and swirling around her.

Above hung two suns, one slightly larger and brighter than the other. The garden smelled of jasmine, lilies, and a tangy scent she might have known in another life. Tiny droplets of water fell on her like stolen kisses, though it was not raining. The droplets whirled and danced and came to rest upon her skin.

A voice called to her from the high branches of an ancient tree. "It's pleasant here, isn't it?"

The voice was deep and gravelly, extremely authoritative, and supremely comforting. Arianna looked up and saw a man dressed in strange, brilliant armors and mail, a sword dangling from his scabbard. His skin was like charcoal, his eyes glowed crimson. Tiny streaks of light raced through his skin.

She knew him. She had always known him. Yet she had never seen him before.

"Come," he said, lowering his hand. Following the movement of the armored man, another branch lowered itself so that she might climb upon it. It was then she noticed her gossamer dress, a bold, striking, rose red.

It was then she felt the crystal dagger in her hand, pulsing, whispering, laughing like the breeze.

The tree bore her up, and soon she was a dozen yards above the garden. A shining city came into view beyond its reaches.

"You've been here before," the man said. "Once, when you were too small to remember."

"I *am* dreaming," Arianna said firmly.

"Of course." The man smiled. "You're not afraid?"

It hadn't occurred to Arianna to be afraid. "Why should I be?"

"You shouldn't. I'm happy you're comfortable here."

"It's like from one of my stories," she said.

He smiled. "Yes, there are many tales of this place, but none, I think, that you would have read. Tell me your tales."

Arianna did. She regaled him with stories of strong young women who rode on the backs of dragons and rescued kingdoms, who fought for righteous causes with swords or crystal daggers like the one she held. She looked down at the weapon and it became mist, fading with a thought.

"The crystal dagger is a gift," the man said. "The first of three."

"But it's gone."

"Never. How can an idea ever truly fade, unless one wishes it to."

"An idea?"

"That all this could be real. Every true thing starts with an idea. Ideas are gifts. You have been given gifts before. Like your strength, and your ability to know what others are feeling, what they will do even before they do. Being different doesn't have to be a curse. Everyone who is special in any way is different. All *heroes* are different."

She nodded, feeling the idea working through her, filling her with a comforting warmth.

"You will be given my second gift when next we meet. Only then, it won't be a dream. We will stand together, in the flesh. Would you like that?"

"Yes."

"The last gift . . . that is something you will have to decide about."

Arianna didn't understand. She said as much.

The man smiled. "You will."

Aurek stirred, groggy from the dream. He lay in a puddle of filth to one side of the Road Eterna, a place visionaries of many worlds had sometimes glimpsed in dreams and called the Rainbow Bridge. Beyond the gutters on either side of the road, reality literally was what one made it: a sylvan forest, a towering city, a shimmering ocean filled with mystical beings. These were not imaginary places. They were shadows, glimpses of a multitude of infinite realities, and imagining called them forth.

They were also *not* for one such as him. Only a sorcerer with a lifetime's worth of experience could hope to venture from the road ahead to one of these lands and not be torn to shreds by the transition from one plane of reality to another. Such an act required far more imagination and skill then he would ever acquire. The human world, however, was a place in harmony with the Seven Realms. A crossing there was possible. He'd done it before, he would do it again.

The filth comprising the gutters between the glowing road and the incredible vistas bracketing it came from the blood and bile of fools throughout the ages who had attempted the journey to the shadow worlds unschooled, unprepared. But it was the only place to rest.

There were challenges on the road, guardians to be won over, bribed, or bested. Only here in this charnel place, this horror, this dark reminder of mortality, could one gain a brief respite. The human lands were far from here, but not so far as they had been. He thought of his daughter and her dreams.

Her fairy tales.

Aurek laughed. *This will be easier than I thought.*

# Chapter Six

Dawn was in hell.

Well, middle school, really. Same diff.

Three days had flown by since Arianna's visit to the Summers household. Dawn had seen the girl at the end of the hall several times and had tried to talk to her, but Arianna always managed to be one step ahead of her, she always seemed to know exactly what Dawn was going to do before she did it; and with that knowledge, Arianna had been able to avoid Dawn with ease. It was one of the powers Buffy said Arianna possessed.

The bell had just rung, and Dawn was hurrying to her locker when she realized she was being followed. The *click-clack* of high heels and the giggling whispers told her it was a pack. A glance at one of the overhead curved mirrors revealed Kirstie and her buddies closing in fast. The Sweater Mafia was putting a hit on her.

Perfect. Just what she needed.

The hall was crowded. Dawn wasn't in a big hurry; she had fifth-period study hall next, and Mr. Miller never said anything to students filing in long after the bell had rung. He was going through a divorce or something and he just didn't seem to care. Bad for him—good for her. She wished Melissa was around to help, but Melissa's grandmother had gotten sick, and her whole family had flown to Florida. Dawn was alone.

She could take herself out of Kirstie's reach by thrusting herself into the rushing river of students attempting to get to their next class on time. That might get her upstairs, downstairs, all the way by the gym, whatever. She could keep watch and navigate her journey just enough to make sure it took her away from Kirstie, and that was what mattered. Then she'd make it back to her locker, then study hall, when the second bell had rung and it was safe.

Cool. She had a plan for dodging the hit.

Suddenly, a wall of big, heavy shoulders rose up ahead of her. A flurry of backpacks and purses and wildly whipping hair cut her off to one side, a freight train of torn jeans slung low, leather jackets, army boots, tats, and piercings the other.

Trapped, Dawn turned, expecting to see Kirstie and her fellow predators standing there grinning, hoping to see fear in the eyes of their prey. Instead, Kirstie and her lieutenants in the Sweater Mafia slipped around her into a gap in the tide of backpacks Dawn hadn't seen. They rushed past her without a single look in her direction, lost in their own little world of vicious or vacuous gossip.

Dawn heard a snippet. Kirstie's best friend talking about her boyfriend. "Then he was, like, oh, honey, I don't even notice any other girls, 'cept to remind myself how lucky I am to have you. . . ."

"Yeah, right, if you believe that," Kirstie said.

"I don't, I just want him to know that I know he's doin' it and he better stop. . . ."

Then they were *gone*. Dawn couldn't believe it. Kirstie and her clutch had been stalking her ever since Parent-Teacher's Night. They were going to get her back, Dawn was sure of that much, and now they were ratcheting up the suspense, playing with her.

Whatever. She didn't have to deal now, and that was all that mattered to her. Dawn found an opening in the crowd surging around the jarhead jocks and made it to her locker. She had the door open and was putting away a couple of books when she heard voices. Closing the door just a little, she peaked past it and saw James, the guy Kirstie's friend Julie had been talking about. She noticed him checking out every girl who went by, but could have cared less. Rushing, she let her study hall book slip out of her hands. Crouching low to grab it, she saw familiar high heels coming her way. A manicured hand closed over her book.

Dawn looked up as Kirstie snatched her book. Julie was there with her guy, and the rest of Kirstie's cronies from the Sweater Mafia had fanned around her, cutting off any possible avenue of escape.

"Carrie," Kirstie said, nodding at the paperback as she rose. She ran her hand through her home curl job. "Yeah, that creepy Stephen King stuff. Just about right for a scrawny freakazoid like you."

A crowd was starting to gather. The second bell would ring any second now. Then the students would scatter as if a starting gun had gone off and their true race had begun. Any second—

Julie sneered, tossing her long, curly brown hair back. She had a thin, heart-shaped face, with lush lips. A Jessica Alba in training. "And she was adopted, right? Like you?"

"I wasn't," Dawn said firmly. "You don't know anything about me."

"I've seen your older sister. Not much family resemblance there." Kirstie shrugged. "Uh, oh. Now we did it. She's crying."

Dawn's entire body shook, and with Kirstie's command, the tears came. Dawn hated the salty streaks racing down her cheeks, hated Kirstie—and hated herself.

"So, how's your girlfriend?" Kirstie said, leaning in. "That skank, Arianna?"

"She's *not*—"

"Really? Oh, my mistake. Dress like one, act like one—"

"She *doesn't*," Dawn said.

"Maybe now you'll think twice before getting in the middle of stuff that doesn't involve you."

Dawn couldn't take this. The bell. The second bell. Where was it?

The school . . . it was helping Kirstie. It protected those it loved. And she was as malicious as this place. Just as evil.

"You're the skank," Dawn said suddenly. "Arianna's decent. You wouldn't know anything about that, you stupid little—"

Kirstie's face was suddenly close enough for her to smell the predator's minty fresh breath and to see the black pools of emptiness that were her eyes.

Dawn took a step back—and looked down an instant too late. Kirstie foot was positioned so Dawn would trip over it if she moved. She stumbled, falling back into the open locker door, slamming it shut with her head, the world tumbling, leaning to one side, the floor reaching up—

*Crack.* Pain exploded in her skull as she hit the hard floor and a pinwheel of stars exploded before her eyes. The book she'd been holding slid across the floor and was stopped by an old sneaker. No one tried to help her up. Dawn got up on one elbow. Her head was throbbing as she looked up—

And saw Arianna standing there, her foot on Dawn's book.

"Oh, great," Kirstie said. "Now it's Bigfoot, fresh from her appearance on *The Jerry Springer Show*."

Laughter pored from the crowd, but Arianna didn't appear to mind. She crouched, picking up the book, her face betraying no fear, only a strange confidence. The edges of her lips rose in a smile as she reached down and hauled Dawn to her feet. Dawn felt as if her arm were going to be ripped clean off, and muffled a cry of alarm. Then she was set down, clutching her arm.

Arianna passed her the book and strolled forward confidently. Kirstie took several steps back, arriving in seconds at James's free side. Julie looked over in surprise, her hand rising to clutch James's hand, dangling from the arm thrown around her. His body looked tight, the muscles in his cheeks twitching, and he did everything he could not to look in Kirstie's direction.

"Well, look at the two of you," Arianna said.

The bell rang. The crowd didn't break up. This was too good.

Julie was about to say something when Arianna silenced her with an open palm. "No, I don't mean you and Jimmy here. I mean the real lovebirds."

Kirstie started to lean closer to James and stopped herself.

"You know, Julie, you really do have every reason to be insecure," Arianna went on. "Clinging to James like that, trying to own him. But, James, he's feeling walled in, trapped, smothered. He hates it. Kirstie there, she doesn't give him any of that. Other stuff, yeah. Like when they're making out in the back of his dad's van. Like when you can't get either of them answering a page. You know, *at the same time—*"

"You're a crazy little low-rent *skank!*" Kirstie said,

but her hand was on James's shoulder, and she was slipping half behind him, as if for protection.

Dawn watched the scene unfold, stunned as Arianna used her intuitive power. Glancing around, Dawn saw what Kirstie must have been seeing: everyone in the crowd staring at the trio with superiority and contempt.

"It's not true!" Kirstie said. She whirled to face her friend, stepping around James—

And wailed as she tripped over his leg the way she had tripped Arianna and Dawn. She went down hard, with a harpy's shriek, her bag hitting the floor and spilling open, pictures of James and her together at an amusement park spilling out.

Arianna snatched the pictures up and handed them to Julie. "Just thought you'd want to know."

Kirstie was trying to get up now. "Ratty lying little—"

Arianna turned away, her foot closing over Kirstie's hand. Kirstie howled, and laughter erupted from the crowd.

"Sorry," Arianna said. "Sometimes I don't know what to do with those big feet of mine."

In seconds, it was all over. A teacher was approaching, and the crowd dispersed. Arianna guided Dawn around to the back of a set of lockers and put her finger to her lips to motion for silence. James stormed off, Julie and Kirstie both racing after him.

The teacher went right by, shaking his head and muttering.

A moment later, Arianna slid out from hiding, Dawn beside her.

"That was amazing," Dawn said.

With wide, frightened eyes, Arianna said, "Tell me about your sister."

# Chapter Seven

After receiving a call from Dawn in the morning about Arianna's request for a meeting, Buffy gathered with the entire group in the magic shop that afternoon. Giles closed the shop early to avoid any risk of strangers—or worse, people who knew Arianna—seeing or hearing anything about the girl's secrets.

They sat around the table often used for research, Buffy directly across from Arianna and Dawn, Giles, Xander, and Anya to her left, Willow and Tara to her right. Introductions had already been made.

"So," Buffy said, doing her best to sound perky as she looked to Arianna. "I'm glad you're here."

Everyone else echoed Buffy's sentiment, and soon an uncomfortable silence fell upon them once more. After all, what did you say to someone who had the power—according to what Arianna had told Dawn—to read you through your body language, to deduce practically anything about how you were thinking or feeling without saying a word? That was provided, of course, she was flipping some internal switch and turning that power on—and Buffy had no idea if Arianna was doing that or not.

Buffy felt so weird. She and the others had talked about Arianna before she and Dawn had arrived. They had decided on certain ground rules, which made sense considering how skittish Arianna had proved herself to be during their last two encounters: no talk of Anya's former demon heritage; no discussion of friendships or other relationships with vampires, werewolves, and other assorted creatures that were generally seen as prime slaying material. In Buffy's life, there were no absolutes, no actual blacks or whites, just an endless series of gray tones. Hitting Arianna with that little factoid right up front sounded like a surefire way to freak the girl out. Better for now to let her think there were just good guys and bad guys and, depending on what they found out about her today, ease her into all the rest of it. Unless, naturally, Arianna managed to intuit the truth on her own.

Buffy ran her hand through her hair nervously. She was the one who had wanted this chance right from the start, and now that it was here, she didn't know what to say, how to begin.

Arianna saved her the trouble. "So . . . there are *things* in the world that most people have no idea about. Creatures, like in fantasy stories?"

"More like horror novels," Anya said bluntly. She had been a little sulky about losing revenue by closing the store early. "Pretty much every evil you could imagine is out there. Demons, vampires, werewolves, swamp creatures, revenants—"

"Thank you, Miss Gloom and Doom," Xander said, jumping in so Arianna wouldn't be scared off. "But there are good things, too."

"Like, um—unicorns?" Arianna asked. "Or pixies?"

"Oh, I love those," Tara said brightly.

"Like Buffy," Xander said. "And you. Brave, strong defenders of the—"

"Okay, *fine*," Buffy said, cutting him off quickly. That was a place she didn't want to go right now. Being a hero was a destiny that had been thrust upon Buffy, and the last thing she wanted was Arianna to feel like she was being recruited to fight the good fight. "Listen, what's important is helping you understand what these powers are, how to deal with them, and, hopefully, why—and I'm taking an educated guess here—they just popped up out of nowhere."

Arianna nodded, letting out a long, ragged breath.

Buffy stared into her eyes and was certain she saw all the same questions there that had troubled her when her amazing abilities manifested for the first time. It wasn't exactly like looking into a mirror—but she knew that expression of complete wiggitude Arianna displayed at all the new ideas about herself and her world. At least, Buffy thought, that's what was weirding Arianna out. No, not a mirror—but close.

"So, Dawn, don't you have some homework that you can be working on?" Buffy asked. "Y'know, like at *home?*"

"No," Arianna said, trembling, looking afraid but resolute. "Dawn and I talked about this. I want her to stay. She stays—or I go."

Buffy frowned as she looked at her sister. *Why* did she have the feeling this was more Dawn's idea than Arianna's? Hmmm, it *couldn't* have anything to do with the look of pure triumph Dawn was exuding as she rocked in her chair, keeping her expression hidden from her friend, now could it? Naw, it wasn't like Dawn was always looking for any way to get in on as much Scoobiness as she could.

Buffy sighed. If only Dawn understood that Buffy wasn't trying to shut her out, that she just wanted to protect her sister.

Anyway, Buffy clearly didn't have any choice about letting Dawn stay. "Sure. No problemo."

Dawn all but did a Snoopy chair dance.

Willow leaned in. "What's important here is that you feel comfortable and safe. None of us here means you harm. We only want to help."

After that, it became Twenty Questions for the newcomer. Could Arianna describe her power, how it felt when it manifested? How strong would she say she was? Had there been any unusual events in her life before the incident at the Quick Stop, any lesser displays of her abnormal strength, intuitive sense, or rapid healing?

They spoke for a time, Buffy shooting comforting looks Arianna's way and trying to get a sense of how well the girl was handling all this. The last thing she wanted was for Arianna to feel like she was at the center of an interrogation.

"So you can't really control this intuitive power," Giles said. "It sometimes manifests in moments of extreme stress, but not always. You can, at times, activate it at will, but, at other times, it fails you completely. I wonder if some part of that is your subconscious at work. There are times when we would simply rather not know things about other people, and times when the truth of a given situation is too difficult to face."

Arianna shrugged. "I dunno. It felt good standing up to Kirstie today. I've been sleeping really well lately, better than I have in a long time."

"Really?" Giles asked. "This is since the first incident at the convenience store?"

"No, since I went barreling out of Buffy's window," Arianna said, averting her gaze. "Sorry about that."

"No big," Buffy said.

"Well, I suppose that would make sense," Giles said. "You panicked initially, but your intuitive abilities made you realize Buffy only wanted to help, and that you weren't alone. It was a comforting thought that got you through the night and led to your increased confidence by day."

"And your putting the major stompin' on the Kirstienator," Xander said.

"Yes, that as well," Giles said. "I have some questions about your parents, if I may?"

Arianna hugged herself. "Sure . . ."

Buffy had a sense that Arianna was feeling a little uncomfortable being so under the microscope here. "Hey, guys, lighten up. She's not a science project."

Everyone fell silent, and Arianna mouthed a quick thank-you to Buffy.

"Right, right, sorry," Giles said sheepishly. "But this is exciting. You know how I am with mysteries."

"Speaking of which, I've got one for you," Xander said, nodding to Buffy. "How does it feel knowing you may not be the strongest in the land?"

Buffy shrugged. "Who cares? We're all on the same side."

Dawn smiled. "Yeah, maybe we should find out exactly how strong Arianna is!"

"Cool," Buffy said, preferring action to chatting any day. Then she looked at Arianna. "If that's okay with you?"

Arianna actually looked relieved.

For the next hour, Arianna's strength and other physical abilities were tested and cataloged in the back room. It turned out Arianna could bench-press almost a thousand pounds, but she had no super-speed, no inherent knowledge of fight moves; she couldn't levitate—or even walk a balance beam without falling. Yet . . . when the chance came up to spar a little with Buffy, the Slayer found it hard to lay a gloved hand on her. Arianna could read her perfectly and see every move that was coming. One thing she couldn't do was take a punch: The lightest tap laid her out, clutching a bruised chin where Buffy had landed a blow.

"You are going to need some serious training," Buffy said.

"I guess so," Arianna said, still sounding a little disoriented as Dawn helped her to her feet. The bruise faded in seconds as everyone watched.

Buffy was stunned. Her own "healing factor" was nothing like this!

She didn't feel a moment of jealousy, only relief. If, heaven forbid, any of the weird things that liked to hang around the home of the Hellmouth hurt her, she had that much better a chance of getting away without a scratch. Well, a scratch that would last, in any case.

There was nothing in any of the texts Willow and Tara had been poring over to explain the source of Arianna's power, so it soon came back to more questions, most of them centering on her parents. When it came out that Arianna's father had left her mother before she was even born, Willow and Giles started exchanging knowing glances.

Buffy chatted with Arianna and Dawn about school and guys and movies and stuff while Willow and Giles prepared a spell that would tell them instantly if Arianna had demon blood coursing through her veins. Then the time came.

Willow uttered some strange words, and her eyes sparkled. A wind shimmering with crimson and golden stars spun around Arianna and quickly faded.

"All done," Willow said, stepping away and looking a little confused. "All clear."

"See?" Buffy said, smiling warmly at Arianna. "No demon blood. Nothing bad."

"Huh," Giles said. "Well, there are other possibilities as to the origin of her powers that might still have to do with her bloodline."

"Thanks," Buffy said sarcastically. "That's *just* what we were all hoping to hear."

Other tests were conducted, and Buffy told Arianna a little more about the "real" world she faced each night. Then Spike arrived as the sun dimmed and dinnertime approached.

"So, I got your message," he said to Buffy. "Just can't get enough of me, is that it?"

"No," Buffy said. "We have a use for you. A way you can be useful."

"There're all sorts of ways I can do that," he said.

Buffy sighed, took Spike to the back room, and explained the situation.

"Oh, the Tara trick, I get it," he said. "And you don't want me to open my gob about being a vamp. So what'd you tell her, that I'm some warrior under a spell, and that's why I can't hurt a human?"

"Pretty much," Buffy said.

"Playing with fire, if this girl can do all you say she can," Spike said.

"I'll tell her everything when she's ready," Buffy said. "Right now, she could just bolt like she did the other night if we overwhelm her with stuff, and I'm not having that."

"Your call," Spike said.

Buffy led him back out to the main room.

"Oh, look at that," Spike said, strutting Arianna's way. "You expect me to take a shot at a sweet young thing like this, staring up at me with those doe eyes and all frightened of the big bad and such?"

Buffy drew a breath as Arianna tentatively proffered her arm. Everything that was about to happen had already been explained to the girl.

"Well, all right, then!" Spike said, yanking his fist back and whacking her upper arm hard.

"OW!" they both hollered.

Spike stumbled off, clutching his head. Arianna massaged her arm. They glared at each other.

"Her bruise'll be healed by supper," Spike said. "This bloody migraine'll last all week."

He stormed off, then came back around and made a quick, whisper-filled, monetary exchange with Giles for services rendered.

"That rules out a bloodline from any other inhuman race," Giles said as he returned to the round table.

Dawn stood before Giles. "I think maybe it's like in the book I'm reading, *Carrie*."

"A physical manifestation of repressed feelings," Giles said slowly. "Yes, possibly . . ."

"Or we might just chalk it up to 'stuff happens,'" Buffy said. "The main thing is whether Arianna wants our help dealing with this stuff." She turned to the girl. "Well? How about it?"

Arianna's face lit up. "You're serious? You'll train me and everything?"

Buffy seemed surprised Arianna was even asking. It was like she hadn't doubted for a second that Arianna would pass her trial. "Yeah. You wanna?"

Arianna nodded her head frantically.

"I'd put that one in the 'yes' column," Xander said as he hovered over Giles's shoulder. He winked at Arianna. "Don't sweat where this stuff is coming from. Some people are just born lucky."

Giles closed his book. "I'd have said 'gifted.'"

"Special," Buffy said warmly. "You're special, Arianna."

"Each and every one of us is completely and totally unique," Willow said, "just like everyone else."

Soon, Dawn and Arianna were on their way to the pizza parlor up the street while Buffy and the others remained behind to discuss their next move with Arianna.

"I, for one, am feeling major-league relief," Buffy said. She circled, hovered, and paced while the rest of the gang lounged at the round table.

"Oh. That's what that is," Giles said.

"Ha," Buffy said, "everyone with the big funny. Look, no demon blood, one hundred percent human, what's not to love about this deal?"

"How long it's taking Anya to get back with our takeout?" Xander ventured.

"Seems to me we've dealt with the heavy stuff," Buffy went on. "Arianna's cool, there's no threat to Dawn. Now we set up a training schedule. Teach Arianna how to deal with what's happening to her. How to make sure she can avoid the kinds of things we get involved in. How to control herself and not lose it on someone in gym class or after school or whatever."

"Yeah," Xander said, "with super-strength, that could be bad."

"Her strength increased as we watched," Giles said.

"Bench-pressing a thousand pounds? Yes, her temper is something she'll have to be very careful about."

Buffy wrung her hands, and her shoes squeaked as she circled even faster. "This is perfect. Couldn't be better. We'll teach her how not to come across dead bodies in the janitor's closet. How not to get on the bad side of vampire masters. How not to have her high school graduation come complete with one giant-sized Mayor-Snake and a near apocalypse. This is gonna be great!"

\* \* \*

At the pizza parlor, Arianna was chattier than ever. "I can't believe your sister!" Arianna said. "The way she moves, the things she can do . . . and she's so *nice*."

"Uh—yeah, right," Dawn said. "Listen, I got a nose needing powdering, 'kay? Just order for both of us if I take too long. I like everything on mine."

Arianna nodded and had a hard time sitting still as her new friend went off. The moment Dawn turned a corner and vanished from view, Arianna let it all hit her, everything she had witnessed, everything that was happening to her. She trembled with excitement. They were going to train her. She'd be a hero, just like in her stories!

Arianna had never been happier in her life. She couldn't even *imagine* anything bad intruding on her life again after this.

# Chapter Eight

Rain streaked across the night sky as Aurek leaped from a shimmering violet portal and took his first steps in the human world for more than fifteen years. He had bested the last of the threshold guardians on the Road Eterna less than an hour ago, and his sword was still slick with the creature's blood. Now he was in the realm of his daughter—and his destiny.

The dim light of the portal reached out from behind him, flaring long enough to reveal that he had simply traded one stretch of road for another. A chipped, yellow divider sliced across this new road's hard glistening black surface. Beyond it lay another lane, then a muddy ditch yawning toward a stretch of woods beyond. The portal's light faded as its swirling iris closed behind him. It would not open again. He would have to find another way home once he was done.

His daughter's world was wet, dark, and miserable—much as he recalled it from his last visit. He could sense her now without any effort. Blood calling to blood. "Soon," he whispered, confident she would hear him.

Then he felt something—a flicker of their connection, stronger this time, and carrying information that made him feel like a damned fool. Arianna had listened to his advice, all right; she had decided her powers were gifts to be cherished—and she had made friends with a group of *humans* who could actually understand and accept her.

He roared with rage. He needed to coax Arianna fully to the point of renouncing her humanity, not embracing it. If she was to become the Reaver, she would have to be set on a path so dark, so *inhuman,* that she would gladly give up her future, her soul, all ties to her world and this weakness humans called compassion. To get what he wanted, he needed to make her into an avatar of destruction and vengeance. Her new friends would help her to avoid such a destiny at all costs.

So he had a nemesis. This young woman, the Slayer . . . he would have to find a way to turn Arianna against her and all the child's newfound friends. It wouldn't be easy, but what in life ever was?

Light washed over him. A roaring steel transport with blinding bright eyes whipped around a curve, racing toward him like some mad beast.

Aurek recalled his *first* time in the human realm, when the sound and fury of just such a metal creature had made him scramble for the muddy embankment like a frightened animal. This time he drew his sword, held his ground, and used his power. He reached out and felt the mind, the presence, the *emotions* of the human driving the transport. Instantly, he knew exactly what the driver would do.

He laughed as the driver swerved the transport to avoid hitting him. The stench of burning rubber snaked into Aurek's lungs as long panels of steel and glass blurred past and were suddenly set afire by the glare of light from the opposite direction. Aurek glanced over his shoulder in contempt as the transport that had dared to charge him smashed into another metal carriage from the opposite lane. Both whipped and jerked high in the air.

Screaming, grinding, shattering metal crunched and clawed and caved. Glass exploded, and a twisted wreck, two steel behemoths locked in a final embrace, skidded down the road. Lights dimmed and died.

Aurek smelled blood. Sword in hand, he examined the wreckage. The bodies were easy to find, though not all were in one piece.

Not one death. Not one, but *three*. A fortuitous number, always. Only minutes in this world and he had been given an insanely glorious sign. From this day forward, he would bow to no one, not a member of the royal family. And certainly not any of these humans . . . They were intriguing, amusing, but in the end, beneath his notice. His elation faded as he gazed at the long road ahead. The rain beat down on his armor, drumming impatiently. He had been walking for what seemed an eternity. No more.

He found a mead house, "Ruby's" by name, a little over a mile down the road. Many transports were parked outside. He would need one of them and the services of a mortal to drive it.

In the rain swept darkness, he cast a simple glamour. Magic fell upon him, a dark fluttering, a burning, a singing of the dark thing that passed for his soul, then it was done. Now all who looked upon him would see exactly what Aurek wished them to see.

Crossing the parking lot, he stepped inside, wondering what his daughter was doing right now.

\* \* \*

Head down, hair hiding her eyes, Arianna trailed

behind her mother at the mall. She'd read that in certain cultures, a woman who followed any less than six paces behind her master could·be severely punished for such a sign of disrespect. It sounded barbaric on the surface, but there were advantages for the women. For example, it gave them an excuse to be well clear when their volatile lords became enraged and needed someone to vent their wrath upon.

This strategy worked with her mother—most of the time.

Arianna's mother lingered before the window of an expensive clothing store, gazing longingly at a powder blue, satin gown. She raised her hands to her thin, once beautiful, now heavily lined face, and swept her long blond hair back. She posed and preened in her white long-sleeved cotton blouse, stained from work, black pants and black work shoes, a rare smile appearing. She looked as if she were imagining herself in that gown at a ball.

*Good,* Arianna thought. *Let her imagine. Let her think of anything except me.*

Arianna thought of using her intuitive power on her mother, but she was afraid. What if—like Mr. Giles had said—she found out things she didn't want to know? What if, crazy as it might seem, her mother was *holding back?*

Arianna stood at the entrance to a bookstore. The wide, cavernous mouth held several displays that rose up like teeth. One was devoted to the latest book by one of Arianna's favorite fantasy writers.

She felt so good after the magic shop and pizza with Dawn. Like, for the first time, she was becoming a part of something. And maybe her life didn't have to be the nightmare she figured it would always be.

Looking away, praying her mother hadn't seen her

watching, Arianna thought about the book.

There wasn't anything wrong with just looking at it. It was just a book, for heaven's sake. She could bench-press a thousand pounds, but she wasn't free to look at a book?

She glanced back. Her mother was still staring at the dress, lost in her dreams of another time, a better time . . .

With trembling fingers, Arianna reached out and eased a copy from the cardboard display. It was a foolish thing to do. She knew that. Far better to read the book in the library. But she had been waiting for two years for this volume to arrive. The painting on the cover called to her. She wanted to see the battlements of the magical city perched on the edge of a waterfall, ensconced within a cavern of unimaginable size, the light from the cavern's mouth reaching out to the heroic dragon-riders circling the city. . . .

This was what she wanted to be. A hero, like Buffy. Someone special, who was free to do whatever she wanted, whenever she—

Arianna gasped as the book was suddenly snatched from her hand. Whirling, she peered into the furious face of her mother.

"You worthless little ingrate," she spat. "How many times have we had this conversation?"

"I was just—I just—"

Mother advanced on her. The woman's searing eyes were dark blue, almost black. Her skin was spotted, worn, the muscles in her throat ropy, making her look twice her age. "I know what you were doing, wishing you could have some other life, be someone else, somewhere else. That's the thanks I get."

"No," Arianna said, though she knew her mother was right. Did her mother have the intuitive power, too? Is that where Arianna got it from?

No, that made no sense. With power like this, a person could become so much more than a waitress working two jobs. She could learn secrets, be a blackmailer or a spy, manipulate her way into the most incredible positions of power this world had to offer. Her mother had done none of those things.

The woman jammed the book back in the display, tearing the cover a little. Arianna winced.

"Oh, great," Mother said. "Now they're probably going to make me pay for it, not like I've got the money, and it's *your* fault. What's wrong with you, anyway?"

Arianna scanned the store. All the employees were busy. No one had seen. They should go now. Right now.

Mother wasn't going to budge. "Oh, right. Just take off, don't take responsibility for your actions. That's just great."

Arianna drew back, shaking, one hand clutching her arm, her sweater sleeve sliding over her hand, leaving only the tips of her fingers exposed. "I'm sorry."

"Pick it up. You wanted it, you're going to have it."

"No."

Mother's eyes widened in disbelief. "What did you say to me?"

"Please, no one saw."

Her mother shook her head. "Pathetic. You should be reading something useful. Something practical. Some book that might teach you a skill, or drill some sense into that empty head of yours, but that'd be asking too much, wouldn't it?"

Mother's voice was rising, and people were looking now. It was late, five minutes to nine, and the mall was mostly deserted. But they were on the second floor, near the food court, where teenagers were closing things down, and a handful of last-minute shoppers raced around.

"There isn't a book, there isn't a prayer, there isn't

anything in this *life* that could make you anything but the biggest disappointment any mother would have to put up with," the woman said.

Arianna felt her tears gather and tried to will them away. She couldn't.

"Oh, great. Now you're gonna cry. That's just perfect. You couldn't be any more helpless and laughable, could you? I bet you can't wait until you're old enough to move out, but good luck with that, 'cause you won't last five minutes on your own. You don't know anything about the world. Not a damn thing!"

Arianna held herself, her lips pursed, her jaws grinding. She knew why Mother was so angry. It was the dress. The dress she couldn't afford.

She had walked five paces behind. Only five, not six, and this was her punishment. This life. This *hell*.

Her vision clouded as the tears fell and her mother only got *louder*. . . .

Buffy and Dawn were on the escalator, climbing toward the second floor of the Sunnydale Mall, stuck behind a couple who were making out the entire way. The Icky-in-Love Club was not what Buffy needed right now. Not that listening to Dawn was much better.

"It's just a concert," Dawn said. "No human sacrifices, no apocalypses, no demon hordes."

"How do you even know that word, and *please* tell me you meant, like, advancing troops of soldiers and nothing else."

"Come on," Dawn pleaded. "I was reading about that martial art stuff you do. A single blade of grass in the field. Wind comes along. Whoosh. If it bends, it's fine. The wind goes away, and it just stands back up again. If it's stiff and brittle, it breaks. Just cut me some slack. Bend, don't break."

"I don't break. I don't bend. I'm not a blade of grass.

I'm your sister and I'm trying to look out for you."

"Don't you trust me?"

"It's not about that."

Dawn threw her hands up in frustration, nearly spilling half the stuff she'd bought at the beauty salon where they'd both just had their hair done.

"You're impossible!" Dawn said.

"Impossible, but resolute. Oh, look, funny hats!"

Dawn snaked her head around the kissing couple as the second floor rose into view. Her angst attack vanished instantly. "Where?"

The affectionate couple stepped off the escalator. Dawn leaped after them. Buffy strolled off, checking her watch. Dawn stepped in front of her, gaze narrow.

"Funny hats are not something to kid about," Dawn said.

"I know. It's your secret weakness. Made you look, though."

"You just wanted me to quit it about the concert."

Buffy looked down at herself and frowned.

"What?" Dawn asked, setting her hands on the hips of her black jeans.

Buffy shook her head. "I just thought for a second you could see right through me."

"Har."

"Many hars. But we've only got a couple of minutes if you want that lip gloss they were out of downstairs."

"Prioritizing is good."

"I like to think so."

They scrambled toward the department store at the far end of the mall. The food court came into view, along with a small group of gang bangers hanging out at the hot dog stand.

Buffy drew a sharp breath. Bangers always made her tense—especially when Dawn was around. Demons and monsters you could count on to follow certain rules. Only attack in semi-deserted spots, like graveyards or campgrounds, that sort of thing. No automatic weapons.

There were no rules with bangers. This crew wore red hooded sweatshirts, a white spiral pattern on their backs and sleeves and faded blue jeans. Red and white bandannas flowing from their pockets or wrapped around their thighs. Shoelaces were untied.

Buffy didn't recognize them.

Dawn stopped, glancing at the ice-cream kiosk.

*No, no, no, not now,* Buffy thought. She was about to gently slip her arm through Dawn's to get her going—then she heard the screaming. Beyond the ice-cream kiosk, at the entrance to Sunnydale's one and only chain bookstore, an older woman was screaming at her teenage daughter. A manager and two store employees were heading their way. The other two or three shoppers who hadn't cleared out of this part of the rapidly closing mall watched the action. The bangers ignored the scene, their heads lolling lazily, hands stuffed in their pockets, hoods casting their faces in shadow.

"It's Arianna," Dawn said.

Buffy recognized the young woman in the oversized sweater who locked eyes with the Summers' women in horror and shame. Buffy's heart sank.

"Come on," Buffy said. "I'm sure Arianna wouldn't want us seeing this."

"We've got to do something."

"Yeah, right. Like make it worse? This isn't any of our business. Mom lost it with us a time or two, y'know."

Dawn shook her head. "That's not what this is."

Buffy had a sense that something was very wrong. She'd seen Arianna fight for her life. Facing this woman, she looked small. Broken.

But . . . what could she do about it?

A pair of hooded figures blurred into existence before her, cutting off her view of the scene across the food court. A red glow rose from the shadows cast by the hood from hollowed eye sockets. Their heads and hands were almost skeletal, covered only by a thin, translucent skin. They were not bangers at all.

"Slayer meat," the closest demon said.

His friend laughed. "Two orders."

Herding Dawn behind her, Buffy checked her corners, positioned the remaining demons in what would soon be flanking positions, and attacked. Her powerful roundhouse kick swept across the face of one demon, then another, sending both spinning to the floor.

What was going on? Demons *never* attacked in public places like this! True, the food court was practically deserted and the mall was almost empty, but still . . .

"Dawn, table!" Buffy commanded. "Get under it and stay down! Now!"

Her sister scrambled out of harm's way. Another demon advanced from Buffy's left flank. She sent it spinning into a table with an inside crescent kick. A spinning heel kick took down the demon coming in from her right. Then she was facing the whole group again, their red shapes blurring. There were only four demons, but they moved so fast, they were back on their feet almost as quickly as Buffy put them down. Speed demons attacking en masse.

Buffy snatched up a couple of hard plastic trays from a nearby table and used them as shields and weapons as the demons rained blows on her. At first it was like being pounded by eight trip hammers moving at super-speed—then the blows stopped, and Buffy heard the demons gasping for breath.

They were sprinters, Buffy realized, only good for short bursts of speed. Dropping low, Buffy spun in a full three-sixty, kicking the legs out from under her attackers. They went down hard, and she vaulted over them, taking the battle away from Dawn's hiding place and giving herself room to maneuver.

*Weapons, weapons, weapons,* she thought. Well, she was in a food court. . . .

The demons howled as Buffy threw anything she could get her hands on against them: pans, spoons, knives, forks—even a sizzling, hissing fryer basket. Two went down in the first barrage, and the other pair scattered.

Buffy darted toward the narrow end of a short rectangular dining table. A demon sped to the other end, blocking her.

"Thanks," she said. It was *so* nice when they went right for it. Buffy leaped high and landed hard on her edge of the table. The opposite end seesawed up and caught the demon under his chin. With a sharp *crack* he flopped away, dazed. While he was still recovering from the blow, Buffy kicked him through the door leading to the bathrooms.

"Where are all the one-liners?" another demon hissed as he closed in. "There's supposed to be quips and witty comebacks and—"

Buffy delivered a knife hand blow to the throat of the first demon. She felt a breeze behind her. One of the quickly recuperating attackers put his long-fingered, skeletal hands on her shoulders. She sent him flying back with an ax kick, then whirled toward a red blur, thrusting her arm out at what she guessed was throat level. He impacted hard, his feet sweeping forward and flying up in the air as he fell from her, his head striking the ground.

"Not feeling quippy," Buffy said.

She saw red again but this time it was just a little guy floating four feet off the ground to one side of the battle, watching intently. He was wrinkly and demonic, with three eyes and kind of a piggy snout. He wore an elaborate costume that looked like a red Japanese kimono with gold spirals. A white sash was wrapped around his waist, and he scratched absently at a pointed black hat tied with a ribbon under his chin. His oblong sharp-toed feet were covered by sandals. He made no move to join the fray, seemingly content to observe patiently.

The three remaining demons were back on their feet, clustered in a group. It looked as if they were trying to decide who would "dance" with her next. Buffy checked Dawn's position. In the confusion, her sister had taken refuge behind the ice-cream kiosk. Only a few bystanders were peering out from the mouths of stores, and all the food court employees were long gone.

"Okay," Buffy said, trying to buy some time, think of a strategy. "So, one question: How come every time I come up against a new race of demons, monsters, or whatever you ugly little things are, it seems like you've all studied the same forms of martial arts. . . ."

She trailed off, looking around, and saw a Hellboy lighter on the ground. Must have fallen out of someone's pocket, she decided as she sprinted toward Dawn. "Hair spray! Now!"

Dawn had the cap off and held the canister out with one trembling hand as Buffy somersaulted and snatched it from her in mid-flight. She landed, the demons blurring into three perfect points around her.

The lighter raised, Buffy flicked its trigger and heard its little whoosh turn into a *big* whoosh as she opened up with the aerosol. A five-foot-long tongue of fire leaped forward, and Buffy spun, searing the faces of all three speed demons and setting one red hood on fire before they could blur out of the way. Dropping the homemade weapon, Buffy made short work out of the non-burning pair with a series of hard strikes and kicks. Meanwhile, head-on-fire guy ran, arms flailing, toward the ice-cream kiosk where Dawn was hiding.

"No!" Buffy yelled.

He wasn't interested in her sister. Dunking his head into a five-gallon drum of strawberry ice cream, he put out the flames, then stumbled into the waiting, helping hands of the demon Buffy had drop-kicked through the bathroom door. The sprinklers hissed into action, showering the food court as a pair of security guards came racing up the escalator. With high yips and howls, the four demons vaulted over the second-floor railing, landing gracefully below and blurring away. Buffy whirled around. The three-eyed floating dude was gone, too.

Buffy grabbed Dawn and steered her clear of the advancing guards.

"Now you understand why you don't go on patrol with me," Buffy said.

"I *helped!*"

Buffy didn't see any sign of Arianna and her mother. Good. Not only had she managed to avoid having Arianna drawn into the fight, there wouldn't be any weirdness the fifteen-year-old would have to try to explain to her mom.

"So," her sister said, "about the concert . . ."

# Chapter Nine

Dawn found Arianna in study hall the next day and sat down beside her, doing her best to cover up her nervousness. Of course, how she could do that with someone who could literally read you like a book, she didn't know. All she could do was hope Arianna wasn't *choosing* to read her. If Arianna did, there were secrets the girl would discover that Dawn would do just about anything now to make sure she never learned. Particularly the way she had turned the situation with Arianna and Buffy to her advantage, pretty much *using* Arianna to muscle in on a little Scooby action. That had been wrong, and especially hard to live with in light of what Dawn had seen pass between Arianna and her mom last night. Yet . . . it was even harder to come clean about it.

"Tell me you're still talking to me," Dawn blurted out.

"Uh, yeah . . . ," Arianna said. She sounded like she had no idea why Dawn would even ask the question.

"Forget it," Dawn said. "It's just—when your whole life is weirdness, it's hard not to have a little of it rub off."

"You mean those guys who went after Buffy at the mall?" Arianna said.

*Those guys,* Dawn thought. *She didn't see that they were demons. Well, that's good . . .*

Dawn nodded.

"No, I get it," Arianna said. "I mean, I was there at the Quick Stop. I saw Buffy fighting before. I kinda get the Slayer thing, and what it's like for you, too. Sorta."

"Okay," Dawn said, but she really didn't see how Arianna could. She thought of the stuff she had to deal with: waking up at three in the morning, knowing she was alone in the house and the only person she had left was out there somewhere, fighting for her life. Knowing that one day, she might be woken by Willow, or one of the others, and whoever had been sent to give her the news would have that look Buffy'd had when she told her about Mom.

Or waking up and knowing she was free, there was no one there to stop her from doing anything she wanted. Sometimes, she went out and did things. Not good things, either. Taking stuff here. Spray-painting some nasty phrase there. Busting up a little something that looked like it needed it. Just because she could.

She did these things, thinking it would make her feel free. Instead, she felt all the more trapped. Confined by secrets she desperately wanted to share and things she couldn't control.

Dawn was well aware that Buffy always thought she wanted to come on patrols because she thought it was all cool and didn't understand how dangerous it really was. That wasn't it at all. A lot of the time, she just wanted to be there—just in case. Because any good-bye could be the last good-bye. Last night at the mall, scary as it had been . . . at least they'd been together.

"I thought you had class this period," Arianna said, snapping her out of it.

Dawn grinned. "Decided to dodge."

"Won't you get in trouble?"

"I'm pretty good at coming up with excuses. Listen, I got something for you." Dawn slipped a book from between her texts.

Arianna took it, her eyes widening in amazement.

"You were looking at that at the mall. I figured I'd pick it up. Just a little something to say, hey, sorry things have been so weird."

Dawn looked over and saw a pale, trembling hand on the book's cover, tracing the city perched upon the waterfall. Her gaze rose.

Arianna was crying. Her body shook as if she were having a fit. She bit her lip, desperately trying not to sob aloud.

Dawn knew that look. For weeks after what happened with Mom, *she'd* had that look. "Getting you out of here, right now."

Arianna nodded and didn't fight as Dawn grabbed their stuff and snuck them out of study hall.

Arianna wiped away her tears. She felt weak and drained as a brittle laugh escaped her. "I can't even imagine what you think about me right now."

She'd told Dawn everything, sitting here beneath the comforting shade of this towering tree looming over the remains of Sunnydale High School. Being close to this place made her feel . . . weird. She sensed birth and death. Growth, destruction. Beginnings.

Endings.

Arianna had painted a vivid portrait of her home life.

She'd never told anyone. Mother always said what happens at home stays at home. But it didn't always. Look at what happened at the mall. What Mother meant was, *it happens on my terms, everything happens on my terms, in my time, my way. . . .*

Arianna didn't know how much more of it she could take. This book that Dawn had bought for her. A simple act of kindness. This gift with nothing expected in return . . .

Dawn was sitting there, shaking her head, staring at the ground, not saying anything.

"I'd better go," Arianna said, scrambling to her feet, not taking the book.

"What? Wait a minute!" Dawn jumped up and leaped in front of her. "It's all right, it's okay."

It wasn't. It could never be okay.

"I'm freaked," Dawn said. "I admit it. But it's not because I think you did anything. It's not because I think anything, except—y'know, your mom . . . it's complicated. My mom, she never . . . How can someone who's supposed to love you treat you like that?"

*Someone who's supposed to love you,* Arianna thought. "Maybe no one's supposed to do anything. There isn't any plan to things. It's just random. Just the way stuff happens."

Dawn pleaded with her eyes for Arianna to wait, give her time. Arianna had felt that way so often.

"I'm not perfect," Arianna said. "I do a lot of wrong things. I'm probably just—"

"You don't deserve it," Dawn said. "You don't. Don't even think that for a second."

"How do you know?" Arianna asked. She didn't know what was inside her. What made it possible for her to do these impossible things.

She opened her purse and took out a picture she had taken from her mother's room, a photograph of how

Mother looked when she was younger, so radiant and beautiful.

"This is what she was," Arianna said. "But with me around . . . you saw what she looks like now. It's all the worry over me. All the bad things I've done—"

"Bull," Dawn said, looking away from the picture. "All that stuff is about her, not you. I've seen you. You're strong. You're strong and you know it and you don't deserve what's happening to you."

Arianna backed away and nearly fell over the remains of some statue.

*I'm strong,* Arianna thought.

Bending quickly, she picked up the head, arm, and shoulder of the statue and tossed it against a far wall. It shattered, and the wall collapsed.

*Strong.*

An abandoned bicycle, its wheels flat, lay on the ground. Arianna grabbed it and pulled it apart, twisting the metal frame like it was nothing. She hurled it away.

*STRONG—*

Arianna screamed and went on a rampage, tearing through the wreckage, ripping apart anything and everything in her path, shattering glass, pulverizing brick, slicing through metal.

She stopped finally, her rage spent, her hands shaking, her mind on the brink of shutting down.

A noise came from behind her. She whirled—and Dawn took a step back.

Arianna felt a surge of satisfaction. She knew it would end like this. Only—she was in control. She had been free to choose how it would end, and she had found the perfect way.

Dawn saw her now, staring as if she were looking at something beyond comprehension. The look subtly changed, her features becoming set. Arianna decided that

Dawn finally understood her for the monster she was.

All her life, Arianna had felt different. Cut off. Mother said it was because she was ugly and a disappointment and a big nothing. She'd *never* be anything else. How could anyone love her? How could anyone even stand to be around her?

Like *she* could ever have friends or truly be welcomed into a group, a family like the one Dawn and Buffy had gained. There was something inside her, something terrible. Mother had known it and had made her see it and feel it every minute of every day. Whenever she was outside, she felt people staring at her, judging her, disgusted by her.

She didn't know why. She didn't understand what was so horrible about her, why she was different.

Now she was starting to get it. All the horrors inside her were coming out.

She waited for Dawn to run away.

Instead, her friend took a step. Then another . . . coming *toward* her.

In Dawn's hands was the book. Dawn stood on tippy-toes and got right in her face, her pretty features scrunched up determinedly.

"If you don't take this, I'm gonna kick your butt," Dawn said.

She was serious—Arianna didn't need special powers to know that.

Arianna didn't know how it started, but suddenly, they were laughing. Both of them, *laughing* and *crying* and *giggling*. The book was in Arianna's hands, Dawn's fingers brushing hers, lightly, ever so lightly, but with a fiery intensity of total acceptance.

The sunlight washed over them, its brightness and warmth becoming all there was for the most incredible moment of Arianna's life.

The light was love. It was trust.

It was hers—and no one would take it away from her.

Aurek sat in the passenger seat of a classic Thunderbird, the driver he had selected at the mead house, a pretty young woman driving cross-country to "the coast," chatting away about her hopes and dreams, her life "back home," and the state of the world today.

In many ways, the human world had changed a great deal in the years Aurek had been away. Technology had advanced, styles had changed, and people often seemed even more self-involved than he had remembered them.

In other ways, on the most basic and primal levels, humans were just as he had remembered them, with an eagerness about them, an openness and optimism, a frailty he found irresistible. There was something about this race and its *softness* that appealed to him. He looked at these humans and thought, *How easily they break, not just in body but in spirit.*

"So, what's waiting back home for you, handsome?" the driver asked.

She smiled, her attraction to him boldly evident to Aurek, and completely understandable. His human appearance, courtesy of his dark magic, was that of a devastatingly handsome mortal man.

"That depends," Aurek said. "Riches and power beyond imagining if I succeed in my quest. Torment beyond imagining if I dare show my face otherwise."

"Oh. Coming to L.A. to get a movie deal, is that it?"

"Pardon?" Aurek asked, surprised. Did she think he was—what did they call it—an actor? He laughed inwardly. In a way, it was true. He had the performance of a lifetime ahead of him in convincing his daughter how much he truly cared about her as a person—and not just what she could do for him.

And the longer it was taking him to reach her, the harder his task was becoming. Only an hour ago he had traced their connection and lightly touched her spirit, learning, to his dismay, that she was becoming even closer to these humans, now confiding one of her deepest secrets to a child her own age.

He would need to employ patience and great skill to sever the links between Arianna and her humanity—on the day of her sixteenth birthday, when the Herald would offer his daughter her birthright, the power of the Reaver, was fast approaching. And as her mentor, her teacher and adviser, he would, in truth, be the most powerful being in a multitude of dimensions. No longer a slave, more than even a master.

He would be a god.

"Come on, no need for the long face," the driver said. "I know it's rough, but so long as you believe in yourself and you don't give up on your dream, no matter what, so long as you hang in there, you'll make it happen. Trust me, I've got great instincts."

Aurek looked at the redhead and smiled as an exit sign for Sunnydale came into view. As he had watched her manipulate the strange vehicle, Aurek had trained his intuitive sense on her to gain an understanding of how to operate the car.

"I'm sure you have terrific instincts," he said, shifting in his chair, the glamour slowly fading, his eyes burning red coals. "But keep in mind—life is *full* of surprises."

# Chapter Ten

Another day, another fight for her life.

Buffy clung to a rusted fire escape, the hot, blinding glare of the noonday sun in her eyes. A half dozen blue-skinned demons had her on the retreat—and she *hated* that. They'd chased her up and down this narrow alley in the worst part of town for at least ten minutes now.

Fighting them wouldn't have been a problem. She'd have taken them one at a time, all at once, whatever.

They didn't seem interested in fighting. They had whips. Really long ones. They liked snapping them. At her.

A lot.

Buffy had tried talking to them. They didn't understand English. When she thought about it, that really wasn't so weird. In fact, the weird thing was how so many demon races, resurrected demigods, aliens, and other transdimensional nasties actually *did* know the language and even tons of passing cultural references.

Well, in a way, that was all right. It let her conserve her voice for really useful stuff, like hollering in pain every time a whip lashed her, and grunting. With the kind of thing she was doing now, jumping from one fire escape to another, trying to kick in windows that had this weird blue-white light covering them—more magical wand stuff meant to block her retreat, she figured—the grunting, hissing, and creative displays of cursing were really important.

It was hard to get a really solid fix on the exact positions of the demons at any given time, because of the annoying way they leaped around. She'd barely gotten a good look at her attackers before the fight had started.

All female. Supermodel perfect bodies and features—practically a Slayer worthy offense right there—wild, incredibly long black hair braided into cornrows; blue skin; bloodred lips; sharply pointed elf ears; burning white eyes; and Xena-style leathers with shiny silver armlets displaying the same spiral pattern worn by the speed demon bangers who attacked her in the mall.

She'd come down here in the first place with a sketch of that design in her back pocket. Show it around, see if anyone had seen these guys. That was the plan.

The next thing she knew—whip, *crack,* slash, ow—and much with the running and jumping.

At least these six weren't as fast as the speed demons from the mall. But man, could they leap. Crouching Tigger, Hidden Pooh-Bear style leaps.

Not endearing.

At least she had a plan for getting out of this. The tenements on either side of her were only three stories. She doubted that whatever magic they were using to keep her from kicking in windows and escaping through someone's living room or whatever extended all the way across the gap between the buildings. Neat trick, that, if you could pull it off. Not many could. So she was pretty confident she could get out of this if she could just escape the little trap these ladies had set up for her. Over the rooftops and through the woods, to Grandmother's house we go. . . .

*Sss—whppppp! Snap!*

"Ow . . ."

Buffy was swinging, jumping, defying some gravity herself, when she noticed the little demon guy hovering at the end of the alley. This time he wore blue, the color this batch of demons favored, but he still had the same symbol on his robes.

The moment of distraction cost her. A wide noose slipped over her neck and down past her shoulders. It pinned her arms to her side as it was pulled taught, and hauled her straight up a dozen feet.

The demoness at the other end of the rope smiled. Perfect teeth, too.

Evil, pure evil.

Buffy was trying to find a way to free herself when the demoness swung her *hard*. Suddenly, the wall was rushing toward her, ready to swat her like a bug even though she'd never done anything to it.

Buffy squeezed her eyes shut.

*This* was gonna hurt.

"Here's the deal," Buffy said. "They weren't trying to kill me. Just really tick me off."

Buffy's punching bag rocked with the fury of her assault. She still had welts from where the whips had sliced through her clothing and struck her skin. A small gash on her cheek was bandaged and would heal before long. She spun, kicking the bag hard. It wobbled away, and she waited for its return.

*Come on, come on . . .*

Giles stood a fair distance away with Willow and Tara, each looking at entries in ancient tomes. Xander sat with a mess of books at the opposite end of the room, head down, poring over them.

"Well, the demons that went after you and Dawn in the mall are called Baycocks," Willow said cheerfully.

"Uh-huh." The bag swung back. Buffy made it pay for that.

Willow winced. "No idea what they're doing here or why they'd attack out in the open like that, which is really the weirdest part of all of this."

"I guess," Buffy said, thinking about the time Angelus and the Judge attacked right in the middle of that same mall, when there were tons more people around. She'd even used a missile launcher in plain sight of ordinary everyday folk. It wasn't exactly like the bad guys had a rule book they *had* to follow. Every situation was different.

"What about the swirly thing?" Buffy asked.

"That's the technical term," Tara said.

"The symbol can mean a lot of things," Willow said. "What *I* think we're dealing with is the Labyrinth." She cleared her throat. "'The winding shape represents a mystery the initiate can only discover by following its sinuous path.'"

"Initiates? Like pledges or whatever?"

"Dunno," Willow said. "We've dealt with demon frats before. Anything's possible."

"We'll keep looking," Tara said.

"Ditto with the Arianna mystery," Willow said. "Her powers have to come from somewhere . . . and we're gonna find it!"

"So, regarding the attack by the blue women," Giles said. "They were being watched over by the same little fellow from the mall?"

"And they had the same spiral symbol," Buffy said, whacking the bag again. "On their jewelry this time."

"Right."

A commotion rose from where Willow and Tara sat cross-legged, surrounded by stacks of demonology texts.

"Oooh—oooh—oooh!" Willow cried. "Got him! Think I got him!"

She handed Xander an open book. He carried it to Buffy and gingerly held it in her field of vision.

Looking away from the bag for just an instant, Buffy grunted at the drawing Xander held up. "That's our Floating Guy."

Giles motioned for Xander to bring him the book. The former librarian pored over the text and muttered, "Interesting."

"Oh, but you do go on," Buffy said, brutalizing the bag some more.

"Ah, yes," Giles said. "Well, it's called a Nadirline. Vital statistics . . . incapable of telling anything but the absolute truth. Photographic memory. The ability to project whatever they've seen or heard, etc., into willing receptors. Normally mages or psychics, though there is a fascinating reference here to some impressionist film directors from the twenties burning their memories directly onto negatives. Hmmm . . . they serve throughout the demon community as chroniclers and are often used to settle disputes because of their absolute honesty."

"Great," Buffy said. "So all I have to do is grab this Nadir-guy and he'll tell us what's going on."

Giles frowned. "I said they don't lie. That doesn't mean they're particularly gregarious. These demons are very discreet. Grabbing him is one thing. Getting him to talk—"

"I will," Buffy said, pummeling the bag. "This is leading to something, huh?"

"I think it's reasonable to assume that these challenges have some greater purpose," Giles said.

"Someone wants a piece of me?" Buffy asked, hitting the bag with everything she had. "They know where to come."

Giles nodded grimly. "Yes. That, in fact, seems to be the problem. Then there's the matter with Arianna."

"You mean that we still don't know where her power's coming from?" Buffy asked, giving the punching bag a rest.

"Among other things," Giles said. "She's adapting quite well, and I'm not sure it's wise to continue keeping things from her. There's a world out there that she may become a part of whether you want that for her or not."

"I told you before," Buffy said. "This is about giving her a normal life, like she wants."

"Is that what she wants?" Giles asked. "How do you know? Have you asked her?"

"So what do you suggest?" Buffy asked, her eyes becoming slits. "That we take her out on patrol? Give her a weapon and say, here ya go, kill or be killed? How very Watchery of you. It gives me flashbacks to my own childhood."

"Of course I'm not suggesting anything of the kind," Giles said. "But we are training her to fight."

"The better a fighter you are, the more ways you know how to avoid getting in a fight in the first place," Buffy said. "Some British former librarian guy said that, I think."

Giles sighed. "At least consider what I'm saying."

Buffy smiled. "Consider it considered. Now let's get back to chasing down the bad guys."

# Chapter Eleven

Arianna couldn't sleep. Ever since she had turned off her bedroom light and lay on her covers, waiting for her body to cool before slipping beneath them, she had felt wide awake, restless. Anticipation moved through her like a living thing. She had no particular reason to feel so excited. Tomorrow was just another day.

Yet tonight, something was coming. Something was *here*.

Tonight . . .

A rapping at her window made her start. Her window was three stories above the ground. There was no fire escape, no tree or anything anywhere near it. The rapping came again. She turned slowly and gasped at the impossible sight of the figure standing just outside her window.

Fear touched her. She wanted to call out, and yet— *this* is what she had been expecting.

She sat up, pulling her long, oversized T-shirt over her knobby knees. The man hovering outside her window was human. Well, he seemed human until she—(*blinked*—and saw crimson eyes; blinked—charcoal skin; blinked—a human face, black hair, aquiline features; blinked—shining armors; blinked—a rugged build, blue jeans, black shirt; blinked—a sword, a scabbard; blinked—a smile.)

He held out his hand. Trembling, her fear replaced with growing excitement, she went to the window. *This is crazy,* she thought. *He could be anyone, anything.*

No, she *knew* who he was.

"Father," she whispered.

He nodded.

Minutes later she walked with him through a neighborhood she might have feared otherwise at this hour. But the narrow alleyways, the graffiti-strewn buildings, the watching eyes of predators, some human, some not, didn't frighten her; not so long as this man walked at her side.

The shadows seemed to recede as he approached them.

"Is this really happening?" she asked.

She was still in her T-shirt, with old, nearly worn, fuzzy slippers on her cold feet.

"It's really happening," he said. "You know me. You remember the dream, don't you?"

She looked away. "I kind of forgot it. Kind of didn't. Like—it was so real when it was happening, but then I woke up and there was all this stuff I knew from the dream, but couldn't really fix on. Some of it I understood deep down but couldn't put into words. A lot of it was, like—*under* my thoughts."

"I understand."

"How did you do that? How did you get into my dreams?"

"I was far from here, and it was the only way for me to see you."

His form continued to flicker between that of the handsome, but inhuman creature from her dream, and that of an attractive, older man.

"Why are there two of you?" she asked. She had so many questions. . . .

"It's called a glamour," he said. "A simple form of magic. It allows me to stay guarded, to—" he waved his hand flamboyantly "—*blend* with my surroundings."

"You look a little like Antonio Banderas."

"No, the glamour does. The illusion."

She stopped.

Her father turned to face her in a circle of hazy amber light from a street lamp that should have been replaced twenty years earlier.

"If you're my father—"

"You know that I am."

Her throat felt dry. She was terrified of the answer to her next question.

She had to know. "Why didn't you come before?"

"I would have," he said. "I didn't know you existed."

"But that place!" Arianna said. "In the dream, you said I'd been there before."

"When you were inside your mother. I didn't know she was pregnant."

Arianna hesitated. She felt her power to read people rise—then forced it away. He was her *father;* of course he was telling the truth. Using her power on him would have been wrong, an insult. Besides, Mother was the one to blame; she had kept the truth of her existence from him. Mother said her father had run off; he hadn't wanted a kid—especially not one like her.

That selfish witch had denied her so much. . . .

"It was only when your dominant nature began to reveal itself that I knew that I had a daughter," he said. "I heard you call out to me."

*That night,* she thought. *After the Quick Stop, when I was alone in my room.*

Her human instincts told her he was telling the truth.

That was enough. Or—it should have been.

The world suddenly crashed in upon her. She felt light-headed, tumbling toward eternity, the world went silent, dark, color drained from existence, then returned. She swam up from the fit, her body weak, her legs hardly able to sustain her weight.

His hands were on her, holding her arms, so powerful . . .

In a heartbeat, her perceptions were normal again.

"I—I didn't mean to," she said. Her power had flared without her conscious will directing it. But she had forced it back, allowing it to only graze the man before her.

He *had* come a vast distance, fought incredible battles, sacrificed much to be with her. And he was her father. Her power had made that much clear.

It was all she needed to know.

She felt ashamed that she had used her power on this man, her father. It was—

"Understandable," he said. "You don't know me. You don't know anything about me."

"I won't do it again. I'm sorry."

He touched the side of her face. "You don't ever have to be sorry with me."

She was surprised to find salty, stinging tears crowding the corners of her eyes, trailing down her cheek, touching his fingers.

He wiped them away.

"I want to see you as you are," she said urgently. "The way you *really are.*"

He glanced about. The street seemed deserted, but there were lights in windows, the sounds of cars not far off. . . .

"What is it?" she asked.

"Our kind," he said. "We have to be careful."

She shuddered inwardly. "Our kind?"

He stared at her. His glamour cracked like a mirror, revealing his true face, then reformed.

"Wait," she said, reeling under the impact of the implication.

*Our kind . . .*

"You're not human, Arianna. Not entirely. How could you be if you were my daughter?"

Her powers, her gifts, and he was a . . .

"Think of me as a demon if that is what you will," he said. "But that is a hateful, ignorant term."

"No, I—"

"I'm not angry with you. I could never be cross with my child. It's not in my nature."

Arianna had to *fight* to keep her power from seeking the truth of those words.

She won.

This was about trust. She needed to trust him, needed it more than anything in the world.

"Some would call us demons," he said. "In truth, we're simply different. We come from another realm of being. Our appearances are not the same as those of humans. But we're no more inherently good or evil than anything else that has ever lived. We have lives. We have feelings, wants, desires. Some would even say we're special. Certainly you're special to me—and to the Seven Realms."

She shook her head. "My friend Willow cast a spell to see if I had demon blood. I don't."

"Your power is growing, changing, is it not?"

"Yes."

"You don't yet know the full extent of your gifts. Because you are the most important of our kind, you have an ability that is not so easy to quantify as superior strength or healing, gifts all Kiritans share."

"Kiritan? That's my kind? Or my name?"

The Marquis Aurek Kiritan introduced himself. "The special power you possess allows you to blend with the humans. It protects you, camouflages you, disguises the true nature of your blood."

"Proof against magic," Arianna whispered, thinking of a passage from one of her fantasy novels.

"From certain intrusive forms of magic, yes."

"I don't look like you. I don't look anything like you."

"We all have many faces, Arianna. You have yet to learn this firsthand."

"You mean . . . I'll change?"

"If you will it. If you desire it. Otherwise? No. And that is well."

"Why?"

"Humans are often not tolerant of anything that is different. I wish it weren't so. Also, our kind has its enemies, those who would see us enslaved or destroyed. Your humanity and your power keeps you hidden, a precious gift none may steal or tarnish."

"Are you back for me? Are you . . . do you want me to . . . why are you here? Wait," she stammered excitedly. "I mean, I'm glad you're here. It's just—"

He laughed and leaned in to kiss her forehead. "You *can't* offend me. In my presence, you can always be yourself, say anything to me. It's fine."

Her shoulders relaxed. Letting out a deep breath, she crumbled into his arms and cried while he held her.

*No one* had ever made her believe those words. She didn't think such openness possible. Now she did.

They walked that night and talked of many things. Of the shining kingdom that could and by rights should be hers. Of many lands oppressed by a corrupt regime. Of worlds within worlds crying out for a hero.

"It could be you," he said. "But that is the distant future."

Fiery glimmers of morning torched the horizon, and the black sky paled to midnight blue, then violet and softer hues.

Arianna looked up and saw they had come full circle. Her home was before her. "I . . . I—"

"Don't say anything. There is much to think about. You'll see me again. We'll talk then."

"Mother . . ."

His back straightened. He shook his head. "She mustn't know. She won't understand."

"Yes," Arianna said. She was certain of that much. "What about the gift? The second gift? In the dream, you said—"

"Knowledge. You have it now: knowledge of who and what you are, where your power comes from, and the destiny that awaits you, should you choose it."

"And the third?"

He shook his head. "Not yet. We have enemies, and I must make it safe for us both."

She still did not quite believe all he wanted of her, hoped of her. To be a champion? A hero?

Like Buffy?

"You will choose and you will do so with your heart. I have no worries. Go," he said lovingly. "The mortal world is waking. Our time will come again soon."

She kissed his cheek. It was hot like asphalt in summer. His heat warmed the coldness worming into her at the thought of another day in this place, another day with her mother.

"I want to go now," she said.

"No, you just don't want to be here. That's different. If you decide to come with me, you'll have to recognize the things you'll leave behind and acknowledge what they mean to you. You'll have to say good-bye to them. It's not a decision made lightly."

He stepped into the quickly growing shadow at the side of her building. "Go, she is waking."

"I love you," Arianna whispered . . . *thought* she whispered. Maybe she only whispered it in her mind.

A voice brushed her thoughts. *You are more than I ever could have hoped for.*

Elated, she ran upstairs.

Buffy was not in a happy place when she visited the Alibi Room. She'd meant to come by earlier, but Spike tipped her off to a vamp nest that had to be cleared out on the edge of town, and it had taken until now to deal with the last of them. At least the weird Floating Guy hadn't been around. Still, it hadn't left her feeling all show-tuney or anything. More *grrr, arrgh*.

She sighed. What she found at Willie's didn't make her mood any better. The normally subdued atmosphere had taken a hike, leaving party central in its wake. Strobe lights flared as monsters of every description partied and got down to disco hits from the seventies. It was standing room only.

There was horror—then there was this.

She pushed her way through the crowd, brushing past a tarantula lady in a revealing white webbing dress, and a horned satyr in a white polyester leisure suit. They'd both had a few too many and simply stumbled into each other's arms. She saw werewolves, elementals, and tons of scabrous demonic types knocking 'em back.

Buffy fought her way to the bar, edging a plastered Minotaur out of his seat. He thudded to the floor, and she slipped onto his stool. Willie had his back turned as he chatted up a couple of wood nymphs in flowing gossamer gowns. They glowed and sparkled and had fairy-like wings, but their teeth were filed to points.

"What happened?" Buffy asked, shouting to be heard over the music. "The Slayer finally buy it?"

"Close," Willie said, still not looking her way. Then his shoulders tightened, and he turned to face her, a tragically phony smile stamped onto his weasely little face. "Buffy! Hey! What a surprise."

"I'm sure," Buffy hollered. "Let's make this quick. Gloria Gaynor makes me twitchy."

"I hear ya, but the rubes seem to love it."

Buffy grabbed the front of Willie's shirt and hauled him close. His breath wasn't all that it could be. Major yuck.

"What's going on?" Buffy asked.

"Happy hour?" Willie asked.

"At six in the morning?"

Willie looked thoughtful. "That late, huh? I guess I'm gonna start losing the undead clientele soon."

So the party had been going on all night. Buffy smiled sweetly. It made Willie shake with fear.

"Tell me who's behind the attacks," Buffy said. "You know, the 'hey, look, it's the Slayer not doing anything, let's mess with her in a public place and then take off, big funny,'—*those*."

"Ah, yeah," Willie said. "Those. Guys with weird spirals?"

"Gals, too." She looked at the watch on her free hand. "You've got sixty seconds, Willie. Then I start tearing this place down. We're talking prime real estate for slayage here."

"Hey, come on, Willie's is off limits, there's been an agreement since I don't know when!"

"Agreement? I don't remember signing anything." Buffy glanced over her shoulder. "Oh, look. Falling-down-drunk demons. Boy, I bet it would take about thirty seconds—ten—no time at *all* to take them out. The rest of these guys? Same."

"That'd be very bad for business," Willie said.

Buffy's gaze went to her watch again. "Twenty seconds or the floor show kicks off. Your choice. I'm in no mood."

"Okay, okay, okay!" Willie said, extricating himself from Buffy's grip. "Now you can't let it out that I told you—"

"Spill."

"You ever watch the Cable Sports Network?"

Buffy drew her stake. "Vamps, at nine o'clock."

"I'm trying to answer your question!" Willie sighed. "Some of these skeleton looking guys with gang colors came in, laughing it up, bragging about the whole thing. Sound familiar?"

She nodded.

"Listen, someone, I don't know who, came up with this idea," Willie said. "Kind of an Extreme Sports for demons thing."

"I'm listening."

"Take on the Slayer, get some shots in, and get out with your head—or whatever—still attached. They've got this whole crazy point system, different kinds of hits, strikes, I can't follow it all."

"I've become *entertainment?*" Buffy asked incredulously.

"Yeah, it's sorta that way. I don't know, if you want to know more, there's this Verdelot guy. Master of Ceremonies in Hell. They got him set up to emcee the awards show at the end. I'm sure your Watcher guy has some kind of summoning spell or hotline number, whatever, to get in touch with him."

"That's what these people—things—are celebrating?" Buffy asked.

Willie nodded at an enchanted mirror across the room. Images of her battle on the fire escape were still running, though no one was paying attention anymore. It made Buffy think of the Slayer Fest one of her enemies arranged for her when she was still in high school.

"Go figure, what's gonna draw the crowds," Willie said.

Buffy was still taking it in. They weren't trying to kill her. Well, *maybe* they weren't. She didn't understand the scoring yet, but there's no way they'd want things over too quickly. Where's the fun in a fight that ends in the second round?

That opened up possibilities. . . .

"People get bored, demons, too," Willie said. "It all starts with an idea. The craziest thing, don'tcha think?"

Buffy turned away, her shoulders tight, her jaws clenched. She was *grinding* again.

As she left, she saw demons and other monsters noticing her. Some nodded respectfully while others sized her up. More than a few laughed.

Buffy walked out, slamming the door behind her so hard, it popped from its hinges, spun around, and collapsed to the floor. Not that anyone inside seemed to notice.

From the sounds Buffy heard as she stormed down the street, the revelries were just beginning.

# Chapter Twelve

Arianna had been up all night, but she was wired, not tired. Bouncy, even. The time she spent with Father had left her energized. Recharged.

The school day had passed in a blur: the usual boring classes, Kirstie steering *way* clear of her, chitchats with Dawn, and daydreams about magical lands and fantastic adventures that would one day become a reality.

In one night she had gained so much. She had a destiny now, a purpose. A future to look forward to rather than dread.

Big changes. Major-league excitement. Holding back from telling Dawn all about her father and her future had been nearly impossible, but somehow, she'd managed. She wanted to tell everyone at the same time.

It was quarter past four. Arianna had run home after school, cleaned up, paid some bills, and raced all the way to the magic shop. She was breathless with excitement as she burst through the door. Within, the entire group was sitting at the round table, pouring over old books. Even Buffy was there, which was odd. She never did research, so far as Arianna knew. From Buffy's expression, Arianna guessed she wasn't happy about it, either, but she appeared determined, too. Only Dawn looked up. She greeted Arianna with a wave and gestured for her to come on over.

Arianna's exhilaration faded as she sensed that something was very wrong. Tension filled the spacious magic shop; Arianna could feel it pressing against her with hard, invisible hands as she slowly drifted over to the gang. A primal instinct told her to make an excuse and get out of there now. Or better yet, just run. She fought it, telling herself she was just experiencing the usual paranoia.

The fear had her, though. Had she done something wrong? She must have. Otherwise, they would have been getting the back room set up, considering it was her training day.

Dawn tapped a seat beside her. "Come on. We're huntin' wabbits."

"Oh, no," Anya said, gasping with terror. "They're finally attacking, aren't they?"

Buffy looked up slowly, her gaze a narrow slit. "*Demons,* guys. We're up against demons. You remember demons, right? Those things we *kill?*"

Arianna suddenly felt light-headed, like she was going to pass out from the explosion of emotions within her at those words. Her skin became clammy, and it was suddenly hard to breathe.

*Some would call us demons. . . .*

She slid into the chair, barely managing to keep herself from falling flat on the floor.

Arianna felt sick. She covered her face with her hand as Dawn excitedly slid a book before Arianna.

"Isn't this cool?" Dawn asked. "Actual Scoob stuff. They're letting us do Scoob stuff!"

Giles glanced in her direction. "Buffy gained some intelligence last night."

Dawn snorted, elbowing Arianna. "She wishes."

Buffy shook her head. "Concert? What concert? I don't remember any concert . . ."

"Come on, it was funny," Dawn said.

"Yuh-huh," Buffy said.

With a heavy sigh, Giles said, "Information. She gained *information* about the demons who have been attacking her recently. It seems that it's some type of competition, one that is growing more deadly with every round. That's why they've been acting so atypical, attacking in broad daylight and in places where there are civilians around. . . . Each group is trying to one up the last, defying the normal rules of etiquette they live by. We're attempting to find any kind of precedent for this, and some idea of what demons might be involved as the battles escalate."

Arianna nodded and opened the tome they had given her. Its cover was crimson, just like the ink on the pages. Trembling, she took in horrible images of demons tormenting their victims.

*You remember demons, right? Those things we kill?*

"Hey, look at this one," Dawn said. "It's got this, like, straw that comes out of its neck, and it uses it to suck out people's spleens!"

"That's it," Buffy said. "Take the books away from them. I told you it was a bad idea."

Arianna barely even noticed as the tome was yanked away. Dawn sat back, her arms crossed over her chest, her lower lip trembling mock petulantly. "You guys never want to trust me with any of the important stuff. I ought to be free to help."

"Dawn, please," Buffy said softly.

"Fifteen," Willow said, nodding at Dawn. "It's a fun age!"

"I'm fifteen," Arianna said. She felt like she was in a haze. "My birthday's coming up. The eleventh . . ."

"Sweet sixteen," Willow said. "That's great! Are you having a party?"

"No party," Arianna mumbled. "Mother doesn't . . . no party."

Willow reached over and closed her hand over Arianna's, her touch feeling like ice. Her *human* touch hurt, felt like stabbing.

"You poor thing," Willow said. "What if—"

Arianna yanked her hand away so hard, she drove her elbow *through* the back of her chair. "Will all of you just *stop?*"

Suddenly, Arianna had everyone's attention, and not in a good way. She hauled her broken chair back, scraping it loudly across the wood floor.

No one else moved. No one spoke. They sat and stared, stunned by Arianna's actions. And Arianna was stunned as well. Was this *really* how they felt about "demons," about people like her? They might as well be saying, kill first, ask questions later.

Willow was on her feet. "I didn't mean to, I didn't . . . What'd I do?"

Arianna had her head down. She wouldn't look at them. Couldn't.

She did—right into all those confused faces. A sea of betrayal, and they were all equally clueless, especially Buffy.

Arianna decided there was no need to use her power to read people on them. Her father had tried to warn her.

*Humans are often not tolerant of anything that is dif-*

*ferent. I wish it weren't so. Also, our kind has its enemies, those who would see us enslaved or destroyed.*

Yet . . . Buffy had been attacked first by these particular demons—or she kept saying. Arianna thought again about using her power to find out if Buffy was telling the truth, but she held back, fear coursing through her. She might learn more than she wanted to know, more than she could handle. The part of her that was human didn't want to lose the friendship of these people, Buffy and Dawn in particular.

Buffy had *everything* Arianna always dreamed about: a loving family, a man who was like a father to her, friends whom she could trust no matter what . . . and Dawn was the most genuine, the most trustworthy, the most *real* person Arianna had ever met.

Arianna felt like she was being split down the middle, her loyalties to either side of her blood confused and threatened.

"Arianna, talk to me," Buffy said softly. "Tell me what's wrong."

It was all falling apart, Arianna thought. Just this morning, she'd envisioned telling the group about her father and his words, asking Buffy to help.

Never. She could never ask now. Not after this. After what they'd said. Yet . . . it wasn't their fault. They didn't know better—they couldn't. How could anyone born completely human understand what it was like to have the blood of another race running through their veins, let alone the blood of people they had been taught to see as evil all their lives?

"I'm sorry," Arianna said, hanging her head in sorrow, feeling almost completely alone. If only her father were here. . . .

No. Who knows how they might react to the sight of him?

Giles rose. "I think we've all been a bit insensitive here. Arianna's training is important, as evidenced by my former chair, and I'm sure much of *this* is . . . disturbing." He swept his hand over the mountain of occult books.

"Not all demons are bad," Anya said brightly. "Some are very smart. And nice. There's this whole rugby team that I am pretty sure is pure demon, and they're—"

"Let's not give her nightmares," Xander said.

Buffy shoved her book away. "I'm never much for this research stuff, anyway; better to leave it to the experts." She smiled. "You wanna train?"

Arianna didn't know what she wanted anymore.

"I mean, with my life," Buffy said brightly. "There's *always* time for killing demons later. You've killed one demon, you've killed 'em all, right?"

The comment, and the casual way it had been delivered, instantly spun Arianna's sorrow and empathy into pure rage.

"Yeah," Arianna said with an icy fury she only barely restrained. "Let's fight."

Arianna struggled to contain her feelings as Giles lectured and Buffy showed Arianna a new series of moves.

"*Ki* is the Japanese word for the intrinsic energy within the human body," Giles said. "It is the inner power that we all possess but few have learned to harness. These movements are designed to help you tap into it. If you can master what's inside you, you can master anything life may throw your way."

Arianna used her power, absorbing the techniques, storing the information, learning the punches, kicks, and blocks faster than she had learned anything in her life. She now had enough control over her intuitive abilities that she could do this without reading any other information about Buffy's beliefs or feelings. She'd heard quite enough on that score.

"Okay, a little sparring, then we'll see how the great research engine in the other room is doing," Buffy said cheerfully. "Fair enough?"

"Fair would be giving it everything we've got, wouldn't it?" Arianna said, her voice inhumanly even. "Treating every situation like it could be life or death, because you never know."

"Well, yeah . . . I guess." Buffy assumed an opening stance. "Bring it on."

Arianna bulleted through Buffy's defenses. She grabbed Buffy's left shoulder and started to turn her, hoping to expose the Slayer's ribs and give her a good kneeing, but Buffy was fast. The Slayer reached across with her right hand and grabbed Arianna's palm, breaking Arianna's hold.

"Hey, slow down," Buffy said, laughing good-naturedly. "I changed my mind. Enough with the giving it everything you've got. Someone could get—"

Arianna wasn't interested in slowing down. She wanted Buffy to understand how it felt to be betrayed by someone you trusted, to have them act like your life meant *nothing* to them just because they were born different.

Arianna lunged, and Buffy grabbed Arianna's right hand with both of hers. She twisted Arianna's arm behind her back and forced her to her knees, the whole thing happening so quickly that Arianna was down before she was entirely aware of what was happening.

"Come on, what's the deal?" Buffy asked, releasing Arianna and bouncing back to allow her opponent time to get to her feet again. "We're just sparring!"

Arianna faced her and tried to land just one solid punch. Buffy used a left knife hand block and a right hand face punch to counter. The blow made Arianna's jaw ache and snapped her head back.

Buffy looked away. "I wonder how—"

Arianna wasn't done. She delivered a jarring right leg side kick to Buffy's solar plexus, and Buffy went down *hard*, struggling for breath.

Arianna looked down at her victim, expecting to feel triumphant, vindicated, just like one of her fantasy novel heroines who'd just defeated an enemy who really had it coming.

Instead, she felt horrible. The gesture, delivering the sudden and unexpected physical blow meant to make Buffy feel the emotional pain that had been inflicted with the Slayer's words and actions, had proven itself empty and meaningless. She didn't want to distance herself from her humanity like this, she was just so overwhelmed and confused. . . .

From the door, Arianna saw the stares of Giles's and Buffy's friends. The sounds of the escalating battle must have drawn the others, Arianna reasoned.

"What'd you do?" Dawn asked, her face white.

Arianna felt the stares of the others burning through her—and she felt lucky the heat didn't burn her alive. Arianna looked away quickly.

"I'm sorry," Arianna said, kneeling quickly to help Buffy. "I'm so sorry, I was just—"

"I've got an idea," Buffy sat, leaning on the girl for support. "How about we go somewhere quiet and just talk?"

Arianna had tears in her eyes as she softly agreed.

# Chapter Thirteen

**B**uffy walked with Arianna down Main Street. The sky was gray, and thunder rumbled in the distance. The lunch rush was over, and very few cars were on the road. Buffy swung her arms nervously, stopping with Arianna before a store window glittering with diamonds and pearls.

"So," Buffy said.

"So."

Buffy crossed her arms over her chest and rocked on her heels. "Blustery day, huh?"

"Milne," Arianna said.

"Pardon?"

"Pooh and Piglet and Eeyore. He's the guy who wrote the books."

"There were books?"

"A dark and blustery day, that's an Eeyore thing," Arianna said. "I thought that's what you were talking about."

"I've seen the cartoons," Buffy said awkwardly.

They went back to window shopping, passing a computer store, a comics shop, and a boutique devoted entirely to leather goods.

"This is nice," Buffy said. "The two of us hanging out. Nice and good. Good and nice. Good with none of the bad stuff, y'know, *that* kind of good. Which is great, really."

Arianna looked away and wandered up the street to the bus stop.

"If you want, we could do the mall thing," Buffy said, hurrying after her.

Arianna stopped and hung her head. Buffy waited, silently hoping Arianna would tell her what was wrong.

"It's just . . . ," Arianna began. "What Mr. Giles said before, about mastering what's inside you—what if you can't? What if what's inside you is too strong for that, or you just don't understand it well enough?"

"Oh," Buffy said, suddenly feeling terrible. "Listen, you know Giles and the others are still working on trying to figure out where your power's coming from, what its limits are, all that stuff. I mean, you *are* aware of that, right? Nobody's given up; they just haven't found anything yet. And this other thing with these demons just kind of got in the way. I'm sorry about that."

"No, I'm not . . . I'm not worried about where it's coming from," Arianna said distractedly. "Just . . . I really screwed up."

"Everybody screws up. I should have listened to my instincts and not let myself get talked into having you see all that demon research stuff," Buffy said. "I mean, considering how it affected you. But Giles said I had to stop holding things back from you, that you were ready to look at all of it, the stuff we really do."

"I am ready," Arianna said faintly, not the least bit convincingly.

"No, it was a screw up on my part, that's all," Buffy said. "You want to hear more about my screw ups, just ask Giles. I mean, like, anytime. Gets him all bouncy. Like Tigger. Bounce, bounce, bounce. More bounce for the ounce. Bounce and pounce. That's what a Tigger does best."

Arianna just looked at her.

"There were books?"

"Short stories collected into two books, yeah."

"Oh."

The silence got them again. Buffy sat down on the bench. "We really should have done this a long time ago. It's my fault."

Arianna tensed. "Done what?"

Buffy looked up in surprise. "You know, this. Talk. Try to get to know each other as people. The thing is, I keep thinking, 'Hey, I was fifteen once. I was fifteen when this thing happened to me. So I should understand what she's going through. We should be able to relate.' But the reality is—"

"I'm not you," Arianna said.

"No," Buffy said, her face brightening. "That's the *great* thing."

"What?"

"I had all this forced on me. I had this great life. Everybody liked me. Mom and Dad were together. It was *all good.* Then one day I'm, you know, super strong and I've got vamps trying to kill me, and all because I'm the Slayer." Buffy frowned. "How'd I become the Slayer? Did I put out a big ad? 'Fifteen-year-old wants to fight, commit slayage, get two hours' sleep every night, walk around like a zombie, not have a life. Not a normal life, anyway.' The answer is, no, nuh-uh. I just got stuck with it."

Arianna looked away.

Buffy sighed in frustration. "There's so much you need to understand—"

"So when can I train?" Arianna said, the light and determination finally returning to her eyes. "You're right. I need to know more, I need to *learn* more. Especially from you. Y'know, someone who kills demons all the time . . . I've got to be ready to fight."

"Well, isn't that good timing," an icy voice said. "Fighting's exactly what's on our minds. . . ."

Buffy and Arianna turned. They were surrounded by demons, six in all. Three pairs. Each demon bore the spiral symbol. The brutish, hairy guys, covered in thick kinky fur from head to toe, had the pattern shaved into their meaty, body-builder chests. The yellow-green insectoids in ceremonial armor displayed it proudly on their vaulted helms.

The last two, a pair of lithe-bodied demons with matching flowing white hair, twisting foot-long horns jutting from their foreheads, pale shadows for eyes, and a sheen of blue-white mist clinging to their all-over-body ritual tattoos, sported the symbol on the end of their silver staffs.

Buffy checked her corners. Nope, no way out. They'd covered 'em all.

"We're here for the challenge," announced the insectoid who'd spoken first. She knew it was him from his tremulous, tinny voice.

"We're at level three," one of the hairy ones said. He looked at her arms and legs. "That means maiming's allowed. Loss of limb, too."

Out of the corner of her gaze, Buffy saw Arianna tensing, looking as if she was about to spring.

Only one thing for that.

"I'll assume that works both ways," Buffy said. "Just one thing before we get started. Curious. Humor me, *here.*"

With a lightning-fast backward sweep of her arm, Buffy connected hard with Arianna, knocking the wind out of her and sending the teenager crashing through the storefront window behind them.

She heard Arianna land, grunt, and spit out a curse.

*Sorry,* Buffy thought. *For your own good.*

She looked to the demon challengers. "So, you guys, what, all got in a cab looking like *that?*"

They screamed a series of warrior howls, and the fun started.

The hairy dudes turned out to be the fastest, surprising Buffy a little. They lunged at her, and she feinted toward the slowest pair, the brother and sister, husband and wife, whatever and whatever with the staffs. Those things weren't going to do them the first bit of good in tight quarters like this, and considering that's where they put their sigils, she figured the staffs were their weapons of choice.

Good. All sorts of possibilities there.

The hairy ones corrected their course just as the insectoids surged at where they thought Buffy was going to be. She dropped low as the demons all collided, and dove through an opening between two of the startled attackers.

"Oh, come on, I thought this was supposed to be tag team!" Buffy said, rolling, springing to her feet, and delivering a spin kick to the face of Hairy Harry the First, who'd recovered fast and was heading right for her. His buddy nearly grabbed her leg before she could withdraw it. She narrowly escaped his grasp, but had no time to move before he plowed her down with his towering, furry bulk. He drove her to the ground, his arms closing on her body as they sank to the concrete.

He was trying to pin her!

She whipped her arms out, breaking his hold, and brought her knees up as her back hit the sidewalk. Her feet caught his chest, and she kicked up and rolled back, sending him overhead and behind her.

A spiral blade bit into the concrete next to her head, shoring a few locks of her hair. Buffy saw another blade blurring toward her and rolled fast, soon clearing the curb and landing in the street.

People would be coming out of the stores. Innocent people.

And Arianna . . .

Buffy got to her feet as the insectoid twins closed on her. She prayed Arianna would stay out of this.

As pincers clacked and clattered and flew at her like swords, she had an almost perfect certainty that the teenager wouldn't.

Arianna climbed to the wobbly frame of the shattered window, stepping over scattered handbags and the remains of well-dressed mannequins. The owner of the store and two customers had run out the back. A cosmetics girl crouched in the corner by the door, her knees pulled up to her chin, her body convulsing in terror as mascara ran down her face with her tears.

Outside, Buffy was fighting—well . . . pretty much all of them.

At once.

Their movements were so quick, Arianna almost couldn't follow them. The demons punched, and Buffy ducked. She kicked, and her target darted out of the way. Weapons flashed, and one was broken, a staff with that weird spiral pattern. A dizzying flurry of punches, kicks, spins, leaps—and Buffy was grinning ear-to-ear, like she was actually *enjoying* this.

"What's with you guys? This is Main Street. It's broad daylight. You just feeling like fighting and all the rules go out the window? I betcha there are people who won't be pleased with this!"

*How can she joke like that? Is it to cover up that she was scared?* To make the danger seem less real so she didn't just curl up into a ball like the cosmetics girl?

Or—did she love this? She certainly seemed to. All her protests aside, Buffy appeared to revel in battling her enemies, every one was a demon. *Like me.*

*No!* she screamed in her skull. *Not like me! Not like my father, not like me. . . .*

But—if Buffy knew the truth, would she make any distinction? Or was it simply that the only good demon was a dead demon?

No, that was crazy. They did that test back in the magic shop to see if Arianna had demon blood. What would they have done if it had turned out positive? Chop her head off right then and there? Buffy wasn't like that.

And these *things* . . . they were nothing like Arianna and her father. Maybe they were the enemies Father talked about.

Ahead, Buffy was driving her opponents away now. If Arianna hadn't been standing in the storefront window, a good three feet off the ground, she'd never have seen Buffy at all. The fast-moving hairy demons were at the back, letting the misting pair and the insectoids do most of the work.

Arianna got a sense that they were studying Buffy's moves. Or just waiting for her to leave them the slightest opening.

Suddenly, one of them spun on Arianna and raced at her, consuming her field of vision in seconds. He was a big, smelly, hairy thing who became her entire world as his huge hand closed on her throat and he lifted her out of the window. His eyes were completely black; his ears pointed and curved outward; his small, perfect teeth so white, they practically glowed as he grinned down at her.

"She was protecting this one," he hissed at his companion, his gaze never wavering from hers. "Breaking her should distract the Slayer."

Arianna couldn't breathe. Fire exploded in her lungs, and she kicked and clawed and struggled like any fragile human being picked off the street might. She didn't act like a hero, she didn't feel like a hero. In that moment, she was certain that she wasn't someone befitting a great destiny like the one Father had hinted at. In fact, if he saw her now, he'd probably be ashamed. It was all lost, tossed away; there was just pain and fear and sweat and reason— reason was *gone*—(she was nothing nothing nothing)

She heard a sharp *crack* and the demon released her. Arianna fell to the ground and saw the monster dropping away from her, clutching the side of his chest, gasping for breath.

Arianna's power flared as she sat up. Her *awareness,* her instincts, roaring to life, telling her the hair ball had broken ribs on top of the compound leg fracture. But how?

She thought of her struggling, her hitting and clawing and kicking and—

Her *strength*.

The other hairy demon flung himself at Arianna. She tried to put her fear aside, tried to remember everything she'd learned in training.

Couldn't.

Instead, she let the world fall into a vacuum, the sounds and colors of reality draining away, replaced with an instinctive understanding of exactly how he was going to strike, considering his pose.

He loosed a blurring right hook, but Arianna quickly sidestepped the blow. He came in with a follow-up punch, and she used a knife hand block to deflect it. She was low, almost at eye level with the center of his chest, her feet spread, her weight perfectly distributed.

Head down, Arianna pummeled the demon's ribs with all the strength she had, three sharp hits, right-left-right, a gasp, a shattering, a heavy hand descending to grasp her by the top of her skull, or her hair. Easily dropping back and away from the falling hand, she delivered a right leg roundhouse kick to the demon's head, sending him spinning before he slapped the ground with his face.

Arianna planted one foot on the small of the demon's back, pinning him to the spot, and took hold of his left arm. She hauled it back and twisted, making him shriek with agony. His eyes rolled back in their sockets, and he sagged, the shock of the pain robbing him of consciousness.

A mild breeze at the nape of her neck, the subtle shifting of air, the smell of sweat and all the information the sweat carried (desperation, rage, wounded pride, fear) all this and more conspired to warn her of another attack. She shifted to a spot that felt safe, a few inches to her right, and felt the hair of the first demon who'd grabbed her as it brushed against her skin, softer and more luxurious than she'd expected. He wobbled by, the spiral blade descending, the broken staff in his hands.

He'd meant to kill her.

Split her skull.

Splatter her brains.

She moved fast, barely conscious of her actions. Her knee right to his wounded ribs, his face contorting in agony as he turned her way and fell, her hands connecting with the grip of the broken staff, cold, smooth, and lethal. The demon on his knees, the spiral blade above Arianna's head.

A voice in her head, the cold, cruel voice of her true blood, shouted at her to finish it. *Kill him! Prove your worth as a great warrior, embrace your destiny!*

Her senses reached out, and she could taste his tears, see his lips moving and experience his terror as he sobbed and pleaded. She had struck at a monster before, at the Quick Stop, but that had been different; there had been no time for thought, only action, no choice but to try to defend herself. But this . . . this would be like murder. No matter what this thing was, or what it had done, she couldn't bring herself to believe it was worth placing that taint on her own soul.

The world suddenly came rushing back, color and sound returning and her power faded on command.

"Get out of here," Arianna said, trembling. *"Now."*

He was scrambling from her, his eyes averted. "Mistress, mistress, be praised . . ."

The demon loped down the street, turning suddenly and disappearing down a narrow alley.

Buffy was *amazed* she hadn't heard sirens by now. Hadn't anyone reported this craziness?

In the heat of combat, she'd seen the two hairy guys break off, their heads bobbing in the background, glimpses of what seemed to be another fight between the two of them. One had dropped from her line of sight. The other had run off, looking totally wigged.

Sheez, a death-duel?

Time to end this.

Buffy sent the closest insectoid flying with a jumping front kick. He sailed ten feet and landed hard, smashing in the hood of a dark blue Buick. Rolling, flopping, and floundering, he fell from the car to the street with a groan and shook his head to compose himself. He looked up and gasped as a Beemer hurtled around the corner.

Buffy heard a screech of brakes, a shriek, and a strangely satisfying thud and splat of impact. The Beemer sped off, windshield wipers attacking the yellow and green muck left behind when the insectoid demon *burst*.

His buddy and the mist-wraiths or whatever they were didn't look so cocky now, even though they'd all proven to be better fighters than she'd expected.

The thing is, there was something else she'd expected, and she didn't want to finish the battle until it appeared.

Floating Guy.

He was there now, in glowing green robes near the mouth of an alley to the store's left. The remaining Hairy Harry had run to one farther down, to the right.

And finally, the sirens were blaring in the distance.

Insect Boy waved an antenna angrily.

"Raid," she said. Couldn't resist.

The male mist-wraith rushed her, his right fist flying at her face. She blocked with a left knife hand block to his wrist and countered with a right knife hand attack to the side of the demon's neck. Grabbing the demon's arm with her left hand and his shoulder with her right, Buffy pulled him down, kneeing him in the ribs with her left knee, then grabbed his head and twisted it, breaking his neck. The body limply fell away. "It's been real and it's been fun," Buffy said. "I think you know the rest."

"Retreat!" The Nadirline called. "The match has ended."

The female mist-wraith didn't look all that broken up about her companion. That was a relief, Buffy thought. She hated when they came back with personal vendettas.

"What about the others?" the female mist-wraith asked, gesturing at the fallen.

"Who cares?" the insectoid demon yelped. "Let's get out of here!"

"No!" the Floating Ref bellowed. "Collect your fallen comrades. Discovery is unaccept—yieee!"

Buffy *liked* that he screamed when she tackled him.

She also liked that there was fear in his eyes as she hauled him into the darkest alley she could find.

It was a promising beginning.

Arianna fell back into the store's shadowy entrance. She could still see the cosmetics girl on the other side of the door, crying hysterically.

The police were coming; she could see blue and red flashing lights down the street.

Suddenly, the mist-woman appeared before her, inhuman and deadly.

"That's mine," the demoness said simply, nodding at the weapon Arianna held.

Arianna handed it back, determined her hands wouldn't tremble—but they did.

Turning, the mist-woman helped the insectoid gather the last of the fallen. Then she sliced at the air with her blade, created a shimmering rift, and helped him drag the bodies through it. The hairy guy stumbled to his feet, ignoring Arianna, and fell through it an instant before it closed.

And, except for a mess on the street that no one would be able to explain anyway, what was left of the insectoid demon who'd been run down by the Beemer, and the storefront damage, it was as if nothing had happened.

Arianna saw the alley where Buffy had dragged the little demon referee guy. She didn't want to know what was happening in there. Not even a little.

Hands in her pockets, Arianna walked on like everyone else as the police cruisers arrived.

\* \* \*

An hour later, in a very private locale, Buffy was calmly reciting plot lines from *Passions* when her enemy broke. She had tried all her usual tactics, including such favorites as using the demon as a punching bag, throwing the guy against the wall, and threatening even worse physical violence again and again, but, as Giles had warned, nothing from her usual bag of tricks worked with this guy. He would endure any physical pain she could dish out, he would die before speaking, Buffy was certain of that, but this maneuver, suggested by a particular platinum-haired vampire who sometimes came in handy, had actually done the trick. By the end, she'd almost felt sorry for the Floating Guy, but desperate times called for desperate measures.

"Yes!" the demon referee wailed. "Yes, I will tell you what you need to know. But you must stop tormenting me so. Poor Timmy!"

"Fess up," Buffy said. "I haven't even gotten to the good stuff. . . ."

The demon shuddered. Tears threatened to burst from all three of his eyes. "The one who came to Verdelot with the original idea is the one you must seek out. His name is—"


*"Spike!"* Buffy hollered as she smashed open the door to the crypt.

He looked up from his telly. "Wot's this, now?"

"It was you," Buffy said. "This whole thing, your idea."

Spike rose from his tomb, awkwardly brushing a pizza delivery box out of the way. "Sure it was. Anything you say. Now, what are we talking about?"

"The Beat-the-You-Know-What-Out-of-the-Slayer-a-Thon?"

"Oh," Spike said. "That."

Buffy sauntered over, hands behind her back, shoulders swinging—and delivered a spinning roundhouse kick that sent Spike flying into the back wall.

Buffy advanced on him—and stopped. "I don't care why, I don't care how, just call it off."

Holding out one hand imploringly, Spike said, "It was just this whole business with Joyce, and there wasn't much going on, and you were looking bad, Buffy."

She waited.

"You looked ready to give it up," Spike said. "I thought, if you had a real challenge, something to keep you on your toes, punching, kicking, making sure those endorphins were doing their job, it might help take your mind off things. Make you feel better."

Buffy spun and kicked in the front of Spike's television.

"Hey, now!" Spike protested.

Buffy ran her hands through her hair. "This is crazy. Here I was thinking you could actually do something about this demon sports mess. Like you have any power."

Spike straightened up, aiming for what might have been dignity, but falling a little short. "Power? You bet I do, Slayer—"

"Defanged, declawed, impotent old Spike—"

"Fine," Spike said, grabbing his coat. "I'll get it done. No more games, the whole thing ends here. All I have to do is put the right word in the right ear—or whatever those disgusting things are on the side of his lopsided head—"

"Verdelot?" Buffy asked. "Tell him for me—"

"I'll bloody well tell him for *me*," Spike said. "I was trying to do you a *favor*, Buffy. Help look after you. I thought that's what she—"

"Not another word, Spike," Buffy said darkly. "Not about her. You don't have the right. She was my family, my life. Not yours."

Spike fixed her with the strangest look. Anger, mixed

with grief, longing, and sheer desperation. It almost made her wonder if she could have been wrong in what she said.

*I know I'm a monster,* Spike had told her once. *But your mother treated me like a man.*

For the briefest of instants, Buffy wondered how well she really understood Spike at all.

Aurek glanced contemptuously at the wounded demon bound beside him in the passenger seat of the Thunderbird. "How's our guest?"

Simply to amuse himself, Aurek poked the frightened demon in his wounded ribs. The hairy thing yelped, but the sound was muffled. A spell of binding prevented him from opening his mouth.

He looked away from the quavering thing. He had been close, so close, to turning Arianna to the darkness she would need to embrace to achieve the full power of the Reaver.

He had followed her when she left school, expending a good deal of his magic to shield himself from her perceptions. He had been outside the magic shop when his daughter had walked in on the Slayer's plans to mount a demon-slaying offensive, and he had felt the girl's anger and confusion—and grinned ear-to-ear when it looked as if Arianna had decided Buffy and her people were the enemy.

Then Arianna had faltered, her human side flaring, all her pent-up desires for love, acceptance, and understanding dousing the fires of her rage. He remained in the shadows when she and Buffy were set upon by this filthy creature and his companions, doing his best to work his will upon his daughter, to make her hear his mental commands to kill this wretch—while believing they were her own thoughts and desires.

Even that hadn't worked. Arianna still wanted to see the Slayer as a noble warrior, a figure to emulate . . . but her resolve was weakening. She had questions that he would have to ensure she gained precisely the right answers to, and concerns about Buffy that he would need to make even more worrisome for the child.

And this captive would play a role in those machinations. . . .

On Aurek's command, the demon sat upright. His arms were bound behind his back, his feet tied together by the same arcane force that kept him silent.

"You're probably wondering what interested me in a lowly wretch like you. It's simple, really. The human you meant to destroy earlier? That was my daughter. I've been keeping watch over her. *She is the Reaver and I am her Keeper.*"

The bound demon went wild with terror, frantically slamming his head on the seat before him as he struggled against his bonds, but to no avail.

Aurek sighed and sat back. "Yes, yes, you've sinned, you've committed a grievous offense against one whose power cannot even be imagined. But I'm going to give you a chance to make it up to her. You have information that should benefit me. I'll allow you to speak, but if you dare say anything except to reveal the nature of this strange competition you and so many other demons are engaged upon with the Slayer, I will make you suffer."

Aurek whispered an incantation, and the demon's mouth popped open. The demon talked. He spoke of his home, of how he learned of the competition, of its rules and scoring, and of Verdelot, who ran the games.

Aurek silenced the creature the moment it began to beg and plead for its life. "You will have to be punished now, but you will be rewarded, as well. Don't worry, I'm sure it will all become clear to you in time. You'll even have another opportunity against the Slayer."

As Aurek watched, the writhing demon's hairy hide grew dark, smooth, the hair falling away as his skin became hard and cracked. Soon, it was charcoal black, with traces of energy racing across its surface. The demon's eyes glowed a dull crimson.

In moments, he would look exactly like Aurek—and soon the endgame would be underway.

Buffy found Arianna sitting on the front stoop of her house. She had *that look* in her eyes. Arianna had done battle, and it hadn't been heroic, it hadn't been fun, it hadn't been pretty. She'd almost died; she might have killed. Buffy had seen that look in the mirror and so wanted to spare Arianna from all the feelings that came with it. "Hey," Buffy said, sitting down beside her. "You wanna talk?"

During the battle, Buffy hadn't seen Arianna, so she hadn't been worried about the teenager. She thought the girl had developed sense enough to run.

No such luck. And this was bad, because she, Buffy, had made a terrible judgment call. She wanted Verdelot's warriors so badly that she didn't prioritize the way she should have. She'd left Arianna alone to face a pair of demons.

Of course, that could happen to anyone, anytime, anyplace. The risk was higher in Sunnydale, but demons got around, and Buffy couldn't be there for her all the time.

Buffy hoped, more than anything, that Arianna had learned from this.

"I couldn't do it," Arianna said. "I mean, I could have. I had them both. They tried to kill me, then I turned it around. I *so* had them, I could have . . . could have done the slaying thing, been a hero like you . . ."

·

Her straggly hair fell before her face as she bowed her head. "I'm nothing. I could have done it, I should have . . ."

"No, you couldn't have," Buffy said. "And you're not *nothing*. You're amazing. You're just not the Slayer. And that's a good thing. We want to help you. We want you to have a normal life, to learn all this stuff so you don't *ever* have to fight like that again."

Arianna looked at her sharply. "You don't understand. It's what I want. I want to be a hero like you."

Buffy was startled. She was certain that she had known what Arianna wanted, and that it was the exact same thing she wanted when her powers appeared. But— she'd never asked the girl. It was like Giles said, about some thing you just don't really want to know, because it's easier to believe what you want to believe. "You don't mean that," Buffy said in a low voice. "You can't."

"Yes, I do! You were fifteen, you were pretty, and you were popular when you got your powers. You were *happy* and you had all that taken away. I never had any of that to start with. This is *giving* me something. And . . ."

"And what?"

Arianna looked away.

"Listen, this hero thing, or whatever, it's not the way it is in stories," Buffy said. "In real life, people die. People you care about *die*. Or they turn into monsters or they go away, leaving you wishing you could just turn everything off and stop feeling. But you can't. And the things you have to do, they change you inside. They make you hard, and before you know it, you're something you don't even recognize anymore."

Arianna was silent, trembling.

"What?" Buffy asked. "What are you thinking?"

Still, Arianna did not respond. Buffy was getting a very uneasy feeling from Arianna. The girl looked like she was making some important decision, and she was doing it rashly. Buffy had been there too many times.

Finally, she looked away quickly, rose, and slowly walked toward the darkness.

"Tell Dawn I'll see her at school," Arianna said.

"Wait—"

"Done waiting. See you around." The darkness took her.

Buffy watched for any sign of Arianna's return. She wanted to go after her. More than anything, she wanted Arianna to understand that all she wanted was for her to have the choice that she had never been offered, the chance to do whatever she wanted with her life.

But that kind of understanding wasn't something she could force on the girl. Arianna was only going to see the truth when she was ready for it, when she chose to do so. And that was one of the choices Arianna would have to make for herself.

Buffy got up and went inside, feeling as if she had fought not only battles, but an entire war today—and lost.

# Chapter Fourteen

Arianna sat on the old swing, her father behind her, gently pushing her in the soft, sweet morning light. He had his "Antonio" face on, but Arianna could see the beauty of his true self behind it. Saturday morning. Mother would sleep until three in the afternoon, easily. If she woke, she'd find the note that Arianna was out taking a walk. She did that a lot. Her mother didn't question it. After all, it's not like Arianna had friends. Or a job. Or a life.

She smiled, her father pushing her higher and higher. The gentle sound of children's laughter rose nearby.

"I couldn't do it," Arianna said. "I couldn't take a life. Not even the life of something like that. I saw what it was, I saw that it would have killed me without thinking twice, but it didn't matter. I just couldn't."

"Taking a life should never be an easy thing," Aurek said. "Far too many treat the destruction of life—or its creation—far too casually. Destroying or creating, it

changes one forever. Killing is a burden that should only
be undertaken if there is no other choice, and the creation
of life a joy, a pleasure, that should only be experienced
when one has earned it. For so many, it is not that way.
You did the right thing, Arianna. Don't let anyone tell
you otherwise."

She swung high, a ridge of treetops rising into view.
"Father—have you ever taken a life?"

The view receded. She sank fast with his silence.
Then he caught her, and placed his hands on her arms.
Despite the morning chill, his hands were warm, even
through the thick fabric of her bulky sweater. He rested
his forehead on the top of her head and slipped his arms
around her, holding her, rocking her gently.

"Yes," he said sadly, wearily. "When it was necessary."

"If I became—what did you call it? The Reaver? I'd
have to—"

"A long time from now," he said. "Maybe never. It
makes no difference."

But it did. She could tell from his voice, *it did.* So
much depended on her, though he wanted desperately to
shield her from that truth.

"What's the third gift, Father?" she asked.

"You're not ready."

"Tell me. Please."

He hesitated. "Power . . . far more than you have
right now. You've been given only a glimmer of what's to
come, if you accept the third gift."

"I want it."

"The final gift comes at a price."

"Tell me."

He released her, came around, and dropped to one
knee before the teenager. His face was grave, yet his eyes
burned with hope, with promise. "Fealty," he said. "Trust.

Believe in what I tell you, know that I would never hurt you, and do what must be done. The power that is yours must be directed."

Arianna closed her eyes. After all she had been through, what her father was offering sounded ideal. Let someone else make all the decisions, bear all the responsibility. But—would it really be that way? When all was said and done, Arianna would be the one holding the sword, the one wielding the power Father spoke of. And, as he said, such things came at a price.

She thought of Buffy and the others, and the price Buffy had talked about. "Those . . . the people I've been spending time with. They kill demons."

"It's who they are," Aurek said. "It's what they do. They can't change their nature any more than we can change ours."

"We're—"

"By their terms, yes," Aurek said. "But do you feel like a demon? Do you think you're evil?"

"Of course not."

Aurek rose and held out his hand. Arianna took it, and they walked together, through the fields they knew.

"Humans use people like us," Aurek said softly. "It is a hard truth, a disappointing one, but difficult to avoid forever. We have talents, special skills. We come in handy."

Arianna listened closely. Talking about this was clearly hard for him.

Suddenly, Arianna thought of the platinum-haired man she'd seen with Buffy the night they met at the Summers home, and again at the magic shop. But he hadn't been around at any other time, and the power he possessed, the way Buffy simply brought him in when she needed to put his skills to work . . . was he a demon, too?

"I don't think they even see us as people." He hesitated,

stopping in a small pool of pure white sunlight. His glamour flickered, revealing his true face for an instant.

Arianna was not afraid.

"I'm not saying all humans are that way." Aurek let out a deep breath. "I shouldn't say all. But there was one . . ."

"Mother."

He nodded. "She thought I was something I was not. A fairy-tale prince, a man who could deliver her from her own wretched upbringing, her squalid beginnings. There were many before me, I found out later. She was very attractive, and she had a way of making a man believe whatever he wanted to believe. If it weren't for you, I can honestly say I wish I'd never met her, never been manipulated by her and hurt by her lies. But—she's given me a gift."

"Like the gifts you've given to me?" Arianna asked.

He shook his head. "I've offered you truth, nothing more. What she's given me . . . you are a miracle, and I say that truly. The pain that was that time of my life, the suffering in the distant past . . . I would sweep it away. I would start again."

Arianna tried to picture her mother with this man— and the thought made her angry. She didn't deserve him. She never could have.

"Perhaps in all this time, she might have changed." He shook his head. "I have to believe it's possible. That all things, in the end, are possible."

"Yes," Arianna whispered.

"You do understand," Aurek said, "who and what I am. One man attempting to do what he believes is right. I'm not perfect. I make mistakes. Even if you became the Reaver and I your adviser, it's possible that I could steer you into something we'd both regret."

"We all make mistakes," Arianna said.

"I try to learn from them. Can you accept me as I am? Flawed, as I am?"

Again, "Yes."

He drew her to him and held her close.

She never felt safer, or more loved, in her life.

Buffy walked the balance beam, pacing across it as if it were just another stretch of floor. She'd reach one end, turn without looking down, and head back again. Giles sat on the bench press, his suit a little rumpled. Dawn was beside him.

Arianna should have been there by now. She was way late, going on two hours already, and Buffy had the terrible feeling the girl wasn't coming at all.

"We're losing her," Buffy said.

"I can understand why Arianna is upset," Giles said, taking off his glasses and cleaning them. "She agreed to the training for one reason, and we agreed to it for another. You want one thing for her. She wants something else for herself."

"Yeah, but she *doesn't*," Buffy said, leaping down from the balance beam and dropping back against it. "She can't."

"Because you don't want her to?" Giles asked gently. "But it's not up to you, is it? As you said, you wanted her to have freedom of choice. That means she may not choose what you want her to, and the more you try to push her—"

"The more you'll just push her away," Dawn said quietly.

Buffy looked at her sister, who had seemed distant, lost in thought, for some time now. It wasn't like her. "What's going on?" Buffy asked. "Dawn, what aren't you telling us?"

Dawn frowned. "There's stuff you don't know.

Nothing to do with Arianna's powers or anything like that. She's . . . I really shouldn't talk about it."

Buffy knelt before her sister. "I know you want to help her just as much as I do."

Nodding vigorously, Dawn clutched at her book bag and held it close. Slowly, she let it down and opened it, handing a small handful of books to Buffy.

Buffy looked at the covers of the three books with surprise and alarm, then lowered herself to a sitting position on the floor and started going through them. They were all on "toxic parents" and the impact verbal and emotional abuse could have, how it scarred a person on the inside the way being hit all the time—or worse—scarred someone on the outside.

"Read it," Dawn said, pointing at the one on the top. "Try, anyway."

Buffy slid the book in front of her and started reading while Giles picked up another and examined it. She had to stop after four chapters. She'd read accounts from survivors of abuse, on the tortures they'd faced, the way some had coped, the way others felt they never would.

A few words on some pages and she felt as if she'd been hit in the gut with a two-by-four.

"Her mother," Buffy said, putting it all together.

Dawn nodded.

Buffy put the book down. The guilt, the anger, the feeling of worthlessness . . . if just reading about this could hit her so hard, what would it be like to live through it? She couldn't even begin to imagine. But now it would be impossible for her to even look at Arianna's actions the same way again. There was stuff she was dealing with that had to be taken into account. The usual standards just didn't apply.

"I don't know what to say," Buffy murmured. She looked up at her sister's wide, soulful eyes and felt her heart break a little. Dawn was growing up, facing demons of a sort that even Buffy had never confronted, and undertaking responsibilities like keeping this secret far better than Buffy might have at her age. She would have allowed herself to express the pride she felt for Dawn, but her emotions had just been dragged through an all new hell.

Buffy shook her head, still trying to process what she had learned. "Dawn, you've carried this around, all on your own . . . I mean—you've known about this how long?"

"Awhile," Dawn said, looking away. Giles set his hand on her shoulder.

"Yeah, awhile," Buffy repeated solemnly. She thought of the scene she had witnessed at the mall of Arianna's mother yelling at her and how she hadn't detected even a little of what Dawn had clearly sensed was going on.

"I shouldn't have told," Dawn said worriedly.

"You did the right thing," Giles assured her.

Buffy sprang to her feet. "I want to get my hands on that woman."

"No," Dawn said firmly.

"She's right," Giles said sadly. "This isn't the kind of evil that you can slay so easily."

Buffy knew they were right, but she couldn't stand by and let this happen. "So—what do we do?"

"It's all about Arianna," Dawn said. "It's about what she chooses. All we can do is make sure she understands we care."

"Wow," Buffy said, genuinely impressed. "When did you go and get all wisdomy?"

Dawn raised her chin and forced a smile. "I have layers."

"That you do," Buffy said warmly.

"Am I wrong, or didn't Arianna say her birthday was

coming up?" Giles asked. "She's going to be—what?"

"Sixteen," Dawn supplied.

Buffy and Dawn exchanged looks. "Sweet sixteen," they said in unison.

"Her mother isn't giving her a party," Dawn said.

"Right," Giles said, "and you both want to do something to let her know she's not alone. She has friends she can count on, right?"

"So we could give her a party," Buffy said, the gears turning in her mind as she imagined it.

"But where could we do it?" Dawn asked.

The Watcher's glasses were in his hand again, and he rubbed at his tired eyes as he said, "The Bronze. There are often parties at the Bronze. A sweet sixteen there, for Arianna, is not inconceivable."

Buffy leaped onto the balance beam. This time, she was excited. "Okay, guys, how long do we have?"

"Four days," Dawn said.

"You've saved the world in less," Giles observed. "Several times."

"Oh," Buffy said with a grin as she looked to her mentor. "*Now* I know who gets to handle decorations."

# Chapter Fifteen

The next three days passed in a flurry of preparation. Arianna had hardly been able to believe it when Dawn approached her about the sweet sixteen party. Dawn took her shopping, made appointments for her at their beauty salon, and helped her pick out an incredible dress. Arianna had objected at first, but what alternative was there? She wanted this party. In fact, she needed it.

At the party, she would say good-bye.

Though no mention was made of it, she would pay her friends back one day. There were kingdoms and riches and incredible adventures in her future as the Reaver. She would return one day, a hero bearing gifts from far-off worlds, everyday trinkets there—items of incredible value here, and shower her friends with them in thanks.

She'd seen Buffy a couple of times along with Willow, Xander, and the others. No one brought up the training, they just talked about the party. There was no pressure, no bad feelings after her blowup the other day. It was like everyone had just forgiven and forgotten, and that would make saying good-bye so much easier.

Arianna still had mixed feelings about what Buffy did and the information she had—and continued—to withhold from her. *Did* the Slayer use demons, as her father had suggested? Would Buffy run from her or, infinitely worse, turn on her if the truth of her demon heritage came out? What other information was Buffy holding back?

It would be a simple matter to gain answers to her questions, Arianna knew; her power could easily make it so. But there were some questions better left unanswered, because so long as Arianna didn't know one way or the other, she could still make herself believe Buffy was a true hero—and a true friend.

And during these days, she had seen the rest of the Scoobs continue to attempt to fathom the true nature and origin of her power. But they were still no closer to the truth, and that was a comfort to Arianna. By the time they knew what was really happening, she would be the Reaver, and she would be far from this world.

There was also no reason to tell Mother about the party. Every reason, in fact, to keep it from her. Arianna had already hidden so much of the truth from the woman, but that was only fair. Mother had done the same to her and worse: The woman had lied to her and made her feel like trash all her life.

Now Arianna had power, she had friends, and she had a father who offered a purpose, a destiny, a chance she'd always dreamed of: to one day *be* something special. . . . Why, then, was she so afraid?

A line from a song came to her. *"When you don't have nothin', you don't have nothin' to lose . . ."*

She wondered why she thought of that now. It was crazy, just crazy. Wasn't it?

Life was wonderful. Amazing. Arianna sat up in her room, in the special quiet of the midnight hours, wondering if she would see her father tonight.

Suddenly, a sparkling burst of flame struck overhead. Arianna wasn't afraid—she'd seen this bit of minor magic before.

The light faded, and a scroll drifted to her hands.

She read the instructions carefully, then set it down and watched as the scroll turned to dust. It had been from Father; he wanted her to meet him.

Arianna slipped out of the apartment once again. Keeping to the darkness, she sped across Sunnydale and stole through the cemetery. Her father told her to meet him there at the entrance to an ancient crypt. Though there had been nothing in the scroll to cause her to fear, she had a sense that his enemies were closing.

*Her* enemies.

*There is one who is a great threat to our cause. One who would take my life in a second if what I planned for you became known. I must deal with this threat.*

*Let me help you.*

*No. For many reasons, no.*

Those words had passed between them just last night.

Pushing branches out of the way, Arianna heard the sounds of struggle. Grunts and thuds. The whisper of steel slicing through the night. A killing breeze.

Edging forward, she saw Father stumble back from the steps of the crypt, his sword held high. Before she could call his name, a shadowy figure surged from the darkness, kicking Father hard in the midsection, doubling him over. He was in a fight for his life. She could sense it, feel his fear, smell his *blood*.

Arianna surged ahead, and something grabbed her leg. The world suddenly dropped and tilted as she was yanked down hard, the side of her skull slamming against a large flat stone. Pain splintered her world, daggers of light ripping through her field of vision. Dazed, her head throbbing, she kicked off the heavy root she somehow hadn't seen, and pushed herself up on one arm.

Ahead, a sword was driven hard through heavy armor with a thick, sucking wet sound. A short cry of agony cut through the night as the sword ripped outward from between the shoulder blades of Marquis Aurek Kiritan, dripping with black blood and bile. Tiny rivulets of soft blue light gathered around the wound, sending sparks flying into the darkness.

Then Father sank to his knees and fell onto his side, his eyes open and staring, his mouth drooling, his chest sinking with a final exhalation of breath.

He was still.

Dead.

Arianna couldn't move, couldn't breathe, couldn't think. Her world was dying. Her future, her dreams, her joy, all fading. . . .

Suddenly, his body burst into blue flame. His murderer leaped back on black high-heeled designer boots and brushed something from her black leather pants. Pulling at the fabric of her tight-fitting turtleneck, she nodded sharply, seemingly satisfied that her wardrobe hadn't been tainted by the blood and bile and bone of her prey. Her leather jacket rustled in the night as her blonde locks cascaded to her shoulders and she tossed them back with a perfect hair flip. In moments, there was nothing left of Father's body.

"Burst right into flames and just turn to ash, why don'tcha," Buffy said. "That's convenient *and* thoughtful. Thanks. I always hate having to bury you guys." She crouched. "Left the sword, cool. Add it to the 'demons I coulda lived without knowing' collection."

Arianna stood silently, desperately wishing this was a nightmare. But it was real. Now Arianna understood the instinct that drove her to run the first time she laid eyes on Buffy. This girl was a killer of her kind; Buffy and her people were the enemies her father had been hiding from. Had Arianna somehow led them right to him? Was it her fault he was dead?

Arianna had no words, nothing she could possibly say to her father's "slayer," no excuses she wanted from the woman, no explanation.

She wanted nightmare. She wanted *death*.

Most of all, she wanted blood.

Her father's words came to her, spinning and cracking and blazing beside the murderous flames torching her reason: *We all have many faces, Arianna. You have yet to learn this firsthand.*

Her flesh changed quickly. She was dimly aware as her soft human skin grew hard and cracked like ancient stone. Her hair shrank back into her skull, and glowing blue and amber light raced across her flesh and fed her (strength STRENGTH *STRENGTH*) with a tingling, intoxicating *rush*. Her body lengthened, her hands expanding to talons, her jaws opening wide and exposing *rows* of sharp, animal teeth.

Her vision changed, but it was different from the other times her instinctive powers kicked in. The night was now bathed in a crimson glow.

Steel-hard muscles shuddered with her every short, quick burst of breath. Anticipation. She was a nightmare now. She was death.

"Someone there?" Buffy asked.

Arianna burst from cover and leaped at the murderer, a scream torn from her soul echoing in the night.

\* \* \*

Buffy raised the sword and raked it across the flank of the *thing* attacking her. It hissed and landed in a roll, springing to its feet and ducking just in time to miss the swing of the sword that might have taken its head. The creature's talons flashed in the night, and Buffy leaped back so quickly to avoid them, she nearly lost her balance. The creature was on her quickly, ripping and slashing, opening up a heavy stinging gash on one arm and another across her thigh.

Buffy drove it back with a swing of her new sword, the biting tip leaving a glowing bright blue wound across its stomach. She scrambled up the stairs of the crypt in a vain attempt to get some height on this thing. Even crouched, it was taller than she was. The creature leaped over her, spinning in mid-leap to avoid another taste of its fallen comrade's sword. A kick to the face sent Buffy's head cracking hard against a stone pillar while a talon gouged across her cheek, neck, and shoulder, splattering blood across the wall five feet away.

Buffy felt weak, tired, and afraid for the first time in a very long time. Her face stung, her head was killing her, and her vision blurred (can't go down, can't give in, can't, got to protect Dawn) and came back into focus. The creature came up behind her, talons whipping through the air. Buffy sent a spinning roundhouse kick to its face, the impact almost knocking Buffy herself back down the steps. It was like kicking stone! She swept the sword at where the demon *should* have been—but wasn't. She compensated for the momentum, found her center, and took in the battleground.

The tomb's small porch was a gray rectangle, ten feet across, five feet wide. Four stone pillars, one at each corner, a door leading into the crypt itself, a stone awning—

*And no demon. Where is it?*

She'd seen it a second ago. A blur of motion, a kiss of displaced air.

Had it gone inside? Or had it leaped down to the clearing, to give itself more room to spring and claw?

A scratching came from above. She sprang toward the crypt's dark hold as an explosive weight struck the awning, shattering it and sending chunks of stone at her with the velocity of pure hatred.

Unlike the one before it, this demon wasn't playing a game. It wanted to kill her, nothing more.

Buffy rolled into the darkness of the crypt and came up fast, the hailstorm of rock still falling without. She held the weapon ready, and felt blood leaking into her eye. Shivering, she rubbed it off with her arm—

And the creature burst in with a roar, catching her at that single vulnerable instant. She swung the sword at its powerful shape, struck *something,* and gasped as the hard impact sent her reeling backward and off balance.

An interior pillar! Not the creature at all. She heard a ripping that might have been someone unzipping a jacket—and felt a biting pain in her back. Falling to her knees, light-headed, Buffy realized it had wounded her again.

The creature vaulted at her and Buffy spun, keeping to one knee, thrusting up with the sword, certain she could impale the demon. Instead, a talon raked across her right arm, the wound deep—

The sword clattered to the ground. There was a hiss, a blur of motion, and a skittering of steel across the floor, and the demon had the sword.

Buffy was losing blood. She had to get out of here *now.*

The demon came rushing at her, the sword awkwardly spinning in its talons. Its glowing blue wounds made the creature look like a blood-spattered nightmare made real, a crimson-eyed, snapping-jawed fiend fresh from the worst hell Buffy could possibly imagine.

She back flipped once, twice, and saw the sword whip down unmercifully, awkwardly, brutally. The door rose up, and Buffy flipped a final time, landing outside, in the mass of shattered stone. Her entire body screamed in fury and pain, desperate for a moment's respite, but the creature was there, the moonlight washing over it, the sword raised high for a killing blow that swept forward—

And smacked hard against the top of the crypt's doorway. The demon was startled—it didn't seem to understand how tall it was, or how to wield a weapon like this.

*Fine by me.* Buffy threw her arms back, swept up several stones, and sent them flying at the demon. They struck the confused creature, impacting hard with its wounded spots, sending it sprawling back into the darkness. Buffy sprang up, stepped in the doorway, and reached inside. Her hand closed over a heavy ring, and she hauled with all her strength, yanking the thick stone door toward her.

The creature within bellowed and raced at her, dropping the sword, launching with its talons. The door closed in its face, the heavy body of the demon helping to slam the door shut. With trembling hands, Buffy dug in her pocket, yanked out the master key she'd stolen from the funeral director's office, and jammed it in the lock.

It turned just as a scraping from the other side of the door sounded and the heavy door trembled with the force of the thing attempting to wrest it open from within. Then came the pounding. The screams. The shuddering and cracking of stone.

Buffy tripped over the broken rocks scattered on the landing, fell down the stairs, and scrambled to her feet, racing to gain as much distance as she could before the creature managed to beat down the door and come after her again.

*Please, no,* she thought, *don't let it have my scent.*

She was halfway home when she looked down and saw how much of the creature's blood had stained her clothing, her flesh. How was it even *alive* after that?

Then she saw her own wounds and wondered if her enemy was thinking the same thing.

At exactly that moment, Arianna burst from the tomb. She scrambled to the ground, looking for blood, reaching out, desperate to catch any trace of the Slayer's fear, any trail that might take her to her prey.

Instead, she discovered only her own purely human terror. Staring down at the bloody talons that had been her hands, Arianna felt her reason return with a jarring impact as her humanity swelled within her.

Murder. Killing. Vengeance.

Blood and pain.

Suffering.

The very subject of the books Buffy and the others had been reading in the magic shop. The tenants of demon lore.

This was not what she wanted, not what she had dreamed of becoming. She had almost taken a life—and she'd almost thrown her own away.

As she watched, her talons receded, her skin softened and paled once more, her hair flowed down and tickled her bloody shoulders.

She was hurt—she felt like she was *dying.* But she knew instinctively that she would live, her body speaking to her comfortingly, her blood telling her all she needed to know.

The wounds would heal. The cuts were deep, but not so deep as to stop her from leaving this place of death and misery.

She felt the cold upon her bare flesh, the piercing whisper of the icy night winds.

Father was dead, his body ashes she could no longer pick out from the filthy soil. And she . . . was an animal, a horrible thing, a creature made for only one thing: killing. That was her destiny, or so it seemed.

Wandering away, she told herself it wasn't true. Father said it would take time for her to become the hero her world needed, and there was a final gift that had not yet been given. Perhaps that gift was what would keep her primal power from overwhelming her reason when she changed, from twisting her into the *thing* she had become.

Only now, with Father gone, she might never know.

Arianna kept moving, toward what she no longer knew, and wept for all she had lost.

# Chapter Sixteen

Aurek watched from the shadows as his daughter stumbled away.

Again she had allowed an enemy to live, and that was not a part of his plan. She should have followed Buffy back to her home and killed the woman in her sleep, slaughtered every human she encountered just for good measure. Instead, she was again *questioning* the demands of her demon blood. Her damnable humanity was putting up far more of a fight than Aurek had anticipated, forcing Arianna to see herself and judge herself by human concepts of right and wrong, of decency and honor.

Even now, Arianna was torn between feeling a need for blood and vengeance—and trying to make sense of what she had seen, trying to come up with some reason other than the obvious one, that Aurek and Buffy were blood enemies—to explain why she had seen the two fighting at all.

He returned to the Thunderbird, desperately searching for some new angle to exploit, another plan that would send Arianna over the edge of reason and into the arms of impenitent darkness.

His plan had been simple enough to sway anyone from my realm: Give his daughter what she wanted, what she'd *dreamed* of having, then snatch it all away. He'd had no doubt at the start of the evening that the sight of his "death" at the hands of the Slayer would be enough to make her renounce her human heritage and embrace the power of the Reaver when the Herald offered it to her on the morrow. No doubt. Creating the illusion was a simple thing, a glamour cast on that wretch Arianna let live the other day to make him look like Aurek, and a simple spell to addle his brain and send him into a berserker's fury at precisely the right time.

It should have been enough to make her snap. But Arianna's ties to her filthy humanity made her resist the call of vengeance and her demon side. He thought she would have left this battle feeling nothing but hatred for humankind, but she still had an emotional connection to her mother, to the Slayer, her sister, and the others. That connection had to be severed. Arianna had to *decide* that human life meant nothing to her, or else she would risk losing the power of the Reaver. Aurek was certain of it.

If she had killed the Slayer there would have been no question of her loyalties, but the child's frail human weaknesses, her remorse, disgust, and self-loathing, had somehow stopped her from continuing on and getting the job done. Now Arianna was questioning everything, seeing her world in an infinite variety of grays instead of the pure black and white he wanted her to view it in. She still lacked the commitment and focus that all the legends said were required for her to earn her birthright.

He had to arrange a rematch between his daughter and

the Slayer—and he had to ensure that this time Arianna would end the battle decisively, killing the Slayer and rejecting all ties to her humanity. Otherwise, his plan might fail, and the consequences would be hideous for him.

Aurek got behind the wheel and cast a spell to make the car drive itself. He had more pressing matters to think about—and an old acquaintance to renew. . . .

Angela DuPrey woke to a pounding at her front door. Her first thought was of Arianna. Why wasn't that stinking brat dealing with this? Angela had had boyfriends come to the door late at night, though not in a while. Bill collectors, too. Arianna knew the drill.

*Worthless child.*

Throwing on her robe, Angela opened her bedroom door. The pounding wouldn't stop and it would soon wake the neighbors. Making a sharp turn, she yanked open the door to her daughter's bedroom.

"You'd better have a good excuse," she said, flicking on the light. "Like, sorry Mother, I was kind of dead, 'cause that's the only reason—"

Angela froze. There was a shape under the blankets, but it wasn't her daughter. She knew exactly how someone rolled up sheets and stacked pillows to make it look, at a glance, like the bed was occupied. She'd done it herself plenty of times when she was young.

Arianna had gone out. She hadn't asked permission, hadn't begged and pleaded and cried like the little wuss she was. No, she'd just left.

From the living room, the front door shook with the power of the blows raining down upon it.

Angela felt a tiny thrill, a little spark of excitement. Inwardly, she denied the pleasurable rush of anticipation she felt at the thought that her daughter had locked herself out and was on the other side of that door, pounding away, knowing the trouble she was in for and desperately wanting to get it over with.

Angela left her daughter's room and strolled to the front door. A song she really liked buzzed around in her mind, and she swayed and bounced a little with the imaginary beat.

Her chest heaved, and she took a deep breath as she stopped before the door. She wasn't a sadist or anything, not like her *own* mother. No, she simply did what needed to be done, keeping her worthless daughter from being any more of a problem than she had to be.

She unlocked the door and hauled it open, ready to give her daughter hell.

She found herself on the receiving end, instead.

Aurek forced his way into the apartment, driving his former lover back with a shove. Angela stumbled over the leg of a chair and fell to the floor.

He closed the door, locked it, and released the glamour making him look human. Then he stood before her as she had once known him: armored, with glowing red eyes, charred black flesh, rivulets of power racing through his skin.

If only this new charade were not necessary. He would have enjoyed rending the woman's flesh. She had aged, becoming grotesque, an affront to a somewhat pleasant memory he'd held for many years.

But he could not risk going to Arianna now. Even if he cloaked himself in the strongest glamour he could manage, she would only have to cast a slim portion of her power at him to see through the disguise. He'd considered using Caroline as his messenger, but she meant nothing to Arianna, and the enchantments binding and wracking her spirit might also be discovered. A willing accomplice was the only way to enact his final plan.

"We have a lot to talk about," he said. "Old times that were not so good. The future, though . . . there's something in it for each of us."

He caught the scampering, frightened animal he had once used for his pleasure by the arm and hauled her up. He barely had to use his intuitive power to know exactly what to say to her. "You knew this day would come, Angela. In fact, you prayed for it. Why else would you have kept the child? And why else would you have tried so many times to get word to me?"

He had known none of this until a moment ago. She had always been easy to read, and tonight she was easier than ever. Though she was quaking, a fragile smile emerged on her haggard face.

"Make me young again?" she asked. "Beautiful?"

"And more," he promised. "You have only to play your part convincingly. It shouldn't be difficult. Now, listen well, there may not be much time."

"How do I know I can trust you?"

A knock came at the door. Aurek reached out with his power. It was *not* his daughter at the door.

"Watch," he said.

He opened the door and smiled at the woman who had come to complain about the noise. Her eyes went wide at the sight of him, and his hand blurred, fastening on her throat and crushing her neck instantly. He yanked her corpse inside and tossed it at Angela's feet.

She didn't seem afraid. Instead, her body relaxed. "Never liked her."

"I could have done this to you," he said. "I have need of you now, I will continue to have need of you in the future. It's about our daughter . . ."

The woman listened, her cruel smile growing as Aurek told her exactly what he had in mind.

* * *

Arianna wandered in a haze, her body clothed in rags she had stolen from the Goodwill dump she'd torn open. Her shape was human again, but the memories of what she'd become, what she'd seen, what she'd tried to do . . . it was almost too much for her.

Her wounds were deep, the pain excruciating. Blood had soaked through the sweatpants and over the shirt she'd taken, and the freezing night wind sliced through her like a thousand rushing blades.

There had to be some explanation for what she'd seen tonight. Some way of making sense of it all.

Her father couldn't be dead, he just couldn't be. She could still *feel* him on some level.

And Buffy . . . why would she do such a thing?

Unless it was as her father said. Humans hated their kind—hated and feared and *used* them, then destroyed them once they served their purpose. He said not all were like that.

Maybe he was wrong. . . .

Confused and alone, unsure of where to turn, she found herself only a block away from home.

The realization hit hard.

Mother.

*Oh, yeah,* she thought sarcastically. *Mother would be understanding. Mother would make it all better.*

Father said he believed all things were possible, and that Mother could have changed.

Arianna set off for the graffiti-covered building. Where else did she have to go? She couldn't go to Buffy or Dawn, not after what she had seen and done. She couldn't trust herself not to become a monster again and kill them both, though, deep down, there was a small part of her, the part of her that was demonic, a part of her she wished didn't exist, that wanted exactly that. Blood and death and vengeance—

*No! I'm human. Human, not a monster. Human . . .*

She found her mother sitting up in her chair, watching as Arianna let herself in and locked the door. The woman was on her feet, racing forward, looking shocked at the sight of Arianna.

"You're *hurt*," Mother said.

"I—I need your help," Arianna said. "It's all gone wrong. It's all gone *wrong. . . .*"

For the first time in as long as Arianna could remember, her mother listened to her. She led her daughter into the bathroom, tended to her wounds, washed her, gave her new clothes—*her* clothes—and listened.

It was nearly an hour later that Arianna saw the glow rising from her mother's flesh. The woman didn't seem tired, for once, or irritable. Her wrinkles and the lines in her face had receded slightly. Her hair had a sheen it hadn't displayed in a decade, and she seemed vibrant in every way.

"He was here," Mother said excitedly. "Your father. Here. He came to talk to me earlier."

Arianna's power flared, then faltered. Mother was telling the truth. Her instincts confirmed it. But she didn't see any further into the woman . . . she couldn't. Her control over her abilities was nowhere near as absolute as it had been, probably a result of the change she had made, her incredible physical transformation from human to demon form and back, and the weakness washing over her from her wounds.

"I've been horrible to you," Mother said. "I could spend a lifetime trying to make it better, but it wouldn't be enough."

Again, her power surged, this time just a little more powerfully. The world spun, and sound and color faded, and *again* she sensed only truth.

Father had touched the woman and healed her somehow, in body and spirit. All her life, Arianna had craved nothing more than her mother's love and approval, and now she had it. Her mother knew she was special, *knew* it, only . . .

Her mother was talking. Describing when she met Aurek and the wonder she felt at being with him, her joy considering the possibility that she could be a part of his fantastic world, and the pain she'd felt in the wake of their parting.

"I made a mistake," Mother was saying, "a terrible mistake. I should have been happy that he loved me. He told me he did, but it wasn't enough for me. I've been so angry at you for so long, and it was for things that weren't your fault. . . ."

Her mother told her that now she understood: Arianna possessed gifts and a heritage her mother could only dream about. Her mother would help her, she would be there for her no matter what. Now, at last, they could be a real family.

Arianna trembled. She had to tell Mother the truth, all of what had happened, the way she had changed, and why. . . .

"He's dead," Arianna said at last, tears flowing freely. "He's gone. I watched and I was so scared, I didn't do anything, couldn't make myself move until it was too late, and his body, it turned into fire. . . ."

Her mother listened. She appeared stricken at first—then her eyes lit up with hope. "There's a way. You can still have the final gift."

Arianna shook her head. "Father's gone. Without his guidance—"

"Wait. Just wait."

She went off and returned with a scroll. "He gave me this spell. If we complete it, we can bring him back to life. He told me to keep it, just in case anything happened to him. In case his *enemies* . . ."

*His enemies. Buffy—and the others.*

Arianna read the scroll. The language was not familiar to her, not at first. But as she stared at the symbols, they began to reconcile in her mind, their meaning becoming clear. Arianna was chilled by what she read. Then she thought of her father's death—and the chill was replaced by fiery determination and rage.

"Slayer's blood," she whispered. "The blood of whoever killed him. That's what we need."

"Can you do it?"

Arianna nodded grimly. Her mother threw her arms around her, sobbing in relief. Arianna tensed at first, then let her own need overwhelm her. She clung to her mother as if she would never let go.

# Chapter Seventeen

"**I** don't know *what* that thing was," Buffy said, flinching as Giles tended to her wounds. They sat in the kitchen of the Summers' home, towels spread everywhere to catch the blood. "All I can figure is this Verdelot guy's cranking up the volume. The rules have changed on the whole Extreme Sports deal, and now they are out to kill me. Final round."

"But there's no evidence," Giles said, dabbing at a gash on her leg with a healing salve. "No sigil on this particular demon, and the referee wasn't present—"

"Not that I saw. I was a little busy."

He shrugged. "It could just be coincidence."

"I don't know," Buffy said. She recalled the look in the eyes of the demon. "I've been in enough fights to know when something's personal. This one—"

A rapping came at the back door.

"I'll get it!" Dawn hollered from the living room.

Buffy frowned. "What's she even—"

Dawn bounded past Buffy in her soft blue flannel robe with Piglet embroidered on the front.

"Why are you up this late?" Buffy asked.

"Cool movie on Showtime," Dawn said. She opened the door and grinned at the figure standing outside. "Hiya, Spike!"

Buffy leaned in close to Giles. "She is way too perky."

"It's the party," Giles replied. "Arianna's sweet sixteen? Dawn is, basically, in charge. The feeling of freedom and empowerment must be—"

"Uh, right," Buffy said, cutting him off. "Spike?"

She slipped her own robe over her taped and bloodied form. "What do *you* want?"

"Ouch," Spike said as she came forward and eased Dawn back. "Looks like something got a piece of you. You doin' all right, Slayer?"

"No," she said. "This little game someone—let me think who'd been enough of a chowderhead to have—oh, right, *you* started, just about got me killed tonight!"

"Not possible," Spike said. "I know those blokes. There's not a demon in Verdelot's legion who could take you. Besides, it's off. What I wanted to tell ya."

Buffy turned to her sister. "Dawn. Bed. Now."

"No," Dawn said with a tiny whine. "There's some stuff to go over for the party!"

"Hey, now, that sounds like fun," Spike said. "Wot, my invite get lost in the mail, then?"

Buffy slammed the door in his face.

"Um—I'll just hang about for a bit, in case you need to talk. . . ." Spike called from outside his voice trailing off, along with his footsteps.

"Rude, much?" Dawn asked.

"We are not having this conversation now." She turned to Giles. "It looks like I'm gonna have to go to hell."

"I coulda told you that," Dawn muttered.

Buffy spun on her. "Bed!"

"This is important," Dawn pleaded.

"Right. And keeping the hordes of hell from our door isn't."

"*That* you deal with every day. Arianna's only gonna have this one day. This one perfect day. If we all work together."

Buffy looked at Giles imploringly.

No help there. She was going in alone. . . .

"Dawn, I can't promise I'll be there. I'll try."

Dawn's mouth dropped. "You'll *try?*"

"I'm gonna be a little busy! Opening dimensional portals, taking on demons on their home ground, figuring out some way of really stopping this craziness once and for all. Yeah, busy."

Placing her hands on her hips, Dawn set her chin a few inches from Buffy's. "You. Will. Be. At. The party. This is not a discussion."

For an instant, Buffy saw her mother in Dawn. She was pleased, moved, and *irked* all at the same time.

"Dawnie, come on," Buffy said. "You know what I have to do. It's not like I have a choice."

"You do," Dawn said. "You can go tomorrow or wait until the next day. There isn't anything that can't wait an extra day or so. That's what you said, when . . ."

Dawn's voice failed her. Tears threatened to burst from the girl as her chest heaved and she turned away, clutching the counter as if she might collapse.

"That's what I said after Mom died," Buffy finished softly.

Dawn nodded. "This is important to me."

Buffy heard footsteps and looked up to see Giles quietly leaving the room. She ran her hand over the back of Dawn's head and eased a few strands of hair away from her eyes.

"I know," Buffy said. "And to Arianna, too."

Dawn turned to her. "You'll be there?"

"With bells on," Buffy said.

Dawn threw her arms around Buffy, hugging her so tight, the Slayer winced and grunted from all the damage she'd taken tonight.

"Oh, no," Dawn said, pulling away from Buffy. Her sister's robe had fallen open, and for the first time she saw how badly Buffy had been hurt. "What happened?"

Buffy closed the robe, tying the sash tighter this time. "You know. Slayer stuff."

Dawn looked away, her shoulders sagging.

"It was . . . it was pretty bad," Buffy said. "I just wanted to, y'know, spare you the gory details."

"Hearing about the gory details, making little sympathetic noises," Dawn said. "Isn't that what being sisters is all about? Part of it, anyway?"

"Part of it," Buffy said.

They sat down and Buffy told her everything.

There were *many* hells, just as there had been many who had, throughout the ages, held the name Verdelot, Master of Ceremonies. Some hells were worse than others, like the hell of Waiting, the hell of Uncertainty, and the hell of Unrequited Desire, all of which were infinitely more torturous than those relying on strictly physical punishment.

The corpulent wretch who now held the name Verdelot, and its attendant duties and pleasures, sat sprawled in a region of perdition that was, for him, at least, the very definition of torment. And not in a good way.

The walls of a great coliseum soared in every direction. Faceless onlookers in crimson robes shook pale, blistered fists in the air as more than two thousand would-be business magnates scurried about the floor of the arena, their black graduation robes billowing behind them as three-headed hell-hounds slashed at them and bit at their heels. The humans clutched their diplomas to their breasts as if they were sacred shields that could protect them from any harsh reality, as if it made them, even now—torn and bleeding, quaking with fear—better than everyone else.

Tormenting the consciences of MBAs was a daily ritual and, ultimately, a fruitless exercise, but what could Verdelot do? He hated being here, but it was a ceremony, and thus, part of the job.

He gestured to the hounds. "Time to take their diplomas. Seize a limb or two in the process, will you? Surprise me. Be creative." He turned away and muttered, "For once."

There were so many more pressing issues to deal with, particularly in the hierarchy of the multitude of regions that comprised hell. Still, he knew he shouldn't complain too much. The sky was black, the birds had been throttled, and the air was filled with the unmentionably putrid scents of blood and waste and fear. And tonight, there was a mixer at Pandemonium, one of the great palaces of Damnation.

All in all, life was good. Still, if only something novel would happen. . . .

"Ahhh!" Verdelot hollered as pain lanced through the bulbous mass that was his skull. He clutched at it with mustard yellow talons, and opened all nine of his violet eyes wide as he tottered to his three-toed feet and swished his tail to free it from his swirling golden robes.

He suddenly felt very cross, and not even the screams from below would suffice to make things better.

A spell of Summoning had just been sent. What's worse, it had to have come from some pathetic mortal, considering the literally painful lack of elegance with which the spell had been cast.

Normally, he would ignore such things. He had *legions* to deal with such minor nuisances, and they were fully free to do so, considering they were no longer engaged in their little competition to see who could best the mortal Slayer. Calling off the games had damaged his popularity a bit, but that filthy Spike fellow had information aplenty that could damage him with his superiors, and so he simply had to honor the vampire's demand.

Verdelot stepped away from the carnage and opened a portal to the coordinates given in the Summoning. He folded time and space, raised all of his mighty chins, and stepped through a portal to the mortal realm.

On the other side, he found himself in a dingy living room, the furniture shoved up against the walls, the carpet rolled up, a human male kneeling in the center of a Protectorate circle lit by flickering candles.

He hovered in mid-air, just for show. "You rang?"

The man abased himself with all the proper rituals of greeting and fealty.

Verdelot was unimpressed. "Tell me your name, child."

"Aurek."

"It is good," Verdelot said, his jaws opening impossibly wide, curved, sharp teeth stretching out to fill the gap. "I always like to know the names of the things I'm about to tear to pieces and consume."

The man's gaze narrowed. "I'm in a circle of protection!"

Verdelot swept forward. "And now, so am I."

Suddenly, the man's form vanished—and Verdelot knew his mistake. A charcoal-skinned demon from one of the many border realms stepped forward. The demon's hands were wreathed in fire. Verdelot felt a sudden urge to retreat, but before he could flounder back through the portal he had opened, an incantation struck him, binding him to the spot. He felt as if a million hooks had dug into his form to hold him. Not altogether a bad experience, but all the potential reasons behind such an act made Verdelot shake with terror.

This was how *he* had ascended to power. Capturing and slaying his predecessor.

The charcoal-skinned demon stepped before him—and changed. The glamour he cast was simple, but effective, and it transformed the demon into a perfect duplicate of Verdelot. "You can choose death, or you can choose to sleep for a time while I use the form I have stolen from you. The choice is entirely yours, and of no consequence to me. The only difference is that if you choose *not* to tell me what I want to know, for whatever reason, understand that I have the power to inflict something worse than death upon you. I can unhinge your soul and send it screaming into the Vast for all eternity. A trick I picked up when I was a child, a minor amusement at birthday parties for such as me."

"I'll tell," the demon whispered.

"Somehow, I knew you would."

# Chapter Eighteen

Dawn Summers greeted party-goers with her usual dazzling smile. The music pounded, and the Bronze was packed. Not everyone was here for Arianna's party, of course, but more had come for just that reason than Dawn ever could have expected.

Still—she was fidgety. She had it on good authority that in the fine art of fidgeting she was second to none. She could annoyingly rap a pencil through an entire class period with the best of them and she could frantically tap her feet to unheard rhythms and bounce and wiggle on top of the fidgeting, keeping track of all of it and delivering it in a single blend of, *oh, yeah, I'm uncomfortable.*

Most of the time, there was no reason for it beyond boredom. This time, she had a rock-solid reason:

No Arianna. Not yet, anyway.

Giles drifted over to her. He looked suitably stylish in his black sweater, she decided. *No stuffiness there.*

"Any sign of her?" Giles asked.

Dawn's smile was the epitome of perky, but her eyes gave away her concern. "Nope. No big, though. She said she wanted to make an entrance."

"I thought you'd be spending the day with her," Giles said.

Dawn sighed, fighting back her worry. "Thought so, too."

"Ah." Giles winced and looked about. "The, uh, decorations came out well, don't you think?"

"Um-hmm," Dawn said. She'd held his hand through the whole process, vetoing his "luau" motif—much to his dismay—and convincing him that what he really meant was the subtle pink and white look that now decorated the Bronze. Pink and white streamers billowed, and pink and white balloons bobbed. On each table lay a pretty cardboard cutout centerpiece with the words SWEET SIX-TEEN. At Arianna's table, a bouquet of metallic sweet sixteen balloons were attached to the birthday girl's chair. On a table safely hidden in the kitchen waited a birthday cake with white and pink icing and sixteen pink candles. Near the kitchen doors, but with full access to everyone, was a table with buffalo wings, mini pizzas, strawberry punch, and more. Another table was set aside for Arianna's gifts.

The Sweater Mafia swept in the room like they owned it. Kirstie looked like she expected a spotlight to fall on her. Heads turned—and that was enough.

"I don't see any signs about this being a private party, so I guess anybody can join in," Kirstie said.

Julie, the girl whose boyfriend Kirstie was cheating with—as exposed by Arianna—was out, a new girl was in, and good old James was there, holding his arm out gallantly for Kirstie. The leader of the Sweater Mafia fixed Dawn with a malicious smile, and Dawn suddenly realized that, of course, Kirstie would look at this as an opportunity for major payback. She hadn't thought of it—and she should have.

The evil clique approached en force—and detoured suddenly as Dawn's pal Melissa slid in front of her. Dawn had no idea she was back!

"Surprise," Melissa said. "Grandma's all better, and I see I've got my work cut out for me."

Dawn was grateful, but this wasn't her buddy's fight. "Melissa, I can't ask you—"

"You're not, I'm volunteering," Melissa said with a little laugh. "It's what friends do. And after what I've been through, watching someone I love go right to the brink and come back . . . it puts things in perspective, and one thing I'm *not* is afraid of that wench anymore. So if I can make Little Miss Thing miserable by keeping her away from you and Arianna, it'll make my night." She winked, and slinked off in her tight-fitting green dress. Heads turned when she went by.

Dawn couldn't believe it. *This is perfect!*

Willow and Tara hurried over. The redhead squealed excitedly. They chatted, Dawn glancing around the club, checking out the time. Where was Arianna?

*And where's Buffy?*

Not far from the stage, Xander danced with Anya. Giles headed their way, saw their intense looks meant only for each another, and zipped off to the punch bowl.

Dawn checked the entrance—and her heart nearly stopped. A blond woman in her mid-thirties strutted into the hangout, chillingly confident in her simple but stylish white silk blouse and black knee-length skirt. A thin black scarf was wrapped around her neck, and her jewelry sparkled.

Arianna's mother—only . . . she looked exactly as she had in that old photograph Arianna had shown Dawn, young and pretty. But that was impossible! What was going on?

Though she hated the idea of revealing Arianna's secrets to even more people, Dawn felt that she had no choice but to quickly get Willow and Tara up to speed.

"Hmmm," Willow said. "Kind of makes the *Carrie* theory about where Arianna's powers come from really look like a winner, don'tcha think?"

"Maybe," Dawn said. But that didn't explain how her mother had been transformed.

Willow's soft, forgiving eyes became dark, hard, and vengeful in an instant as her small hands balled into fists. "Don't worry, Dawn. Nothing's gonna go wrong tonight."

Dawn felt something like electricity in the air, a crackling field of energy pushing against her and lifting her hair. Willow was gathering her magic about her.

"Lady, I'm all over you tonight," Willow said, leading Tara away as they followed Arianna's mother into the crowd.

The music changed suddenly. A song Dawn knew Arianna loved came on, and the lights dimmed.

"You look so fine . . .," a sultry voice sang.

Then a spotlight hit the door—and Arianna made her entrance. She looked like a vision to Dawn. A goddess.

Her long, lean body had been *poured* into a crimson satin dress. Its tasteful V-neck cut accentuated her tiny waist and flared in all the right places to give her a subtle hourglass figure. Her arms were bare, except for a stunning burnished copper wrist cuff adorned with a crimson jewel in its center, and a pair of tear-shaped amber stones pointing above and below. The gown flowed around her as she moved with absolute confidence. Her hair, which had been a stringy, straw-colored mess, was now golden honey and stylishly crimped. Her makeup was unbelievable. She looked like a supermodel.

*Better.*

Dawn wasn't the only one caught with her jaw hanging open. Everyone stared and Arianna appeared to delight in the attention.

Then Arianna was in the room, and party-goers were flocking around her as Xander hurried to Dawn's side, along with Giles. Both were in a state of prepared readiness—Xander with Arianna's corsage, Giles with a camera to capture the event.

Dawn saw that Arianna's eyes were cool as the trio approached. Arianna smiled slightly as Dawn fawned all over her, taking the corsage from Xander's hands and posing, all smiles, for pictures with Giles. Dawn didn't know when or how to tell Arianna her mother was here. She even wondered if she should ask Willow to, well, *do something* to make her go away. Magic up her will or some such thing, make her think it was a great time to wander the mall, anything.

But . . . how had the woman even found out about this? The mother of another student? Someone she worked with? And why did the woman look so different?

Spotting Willow and Tara at the edge of the crowd, Dawn slipped away to talk with them.

"Gone," Willow said, looking confused. "One minute, there, the next, no evil mother to worry about. Right into the shadows and out of the way, and I don't see how that's possible. I was using magic to track her."

"Maybe she was seeing if they were hiring," Tara suggested quietly. "She works at a restaurant. Could be that. And spells, y'know . . . sometimes go ker-plooey."

Dawn wasn't going to worry about it. The woman's disappearance was the best news she could have been given.

"We'll keep hunting for her," Willow said.

Nodding, Dawn went back to Arianna and got the festivities underway. A scavenger hunt Dawn had orchestrated was the first bit of fun for the night.

"The only rule is that everyone has to stay in the Bronze to find the items," Dawn said. "You're looking for sixteen birthday candles, sixteen toothpicks—extra points if they're colored, sixteen matchsticks, sixteen pennies—extra points if they're nineteen eighty-six, the year of Arianna's birth, sixteen cash register receipts, sixteen straws, sixteen signatures of people at the party, sixteen uninflated balloons, sixteen shoes, sixteen hairbrushes, sixteen magazines, and sixteen broken crayons—extra points for a red one, it's Arianna's favorite color."

Then everyone was off. Dawn was thrilled to see how many people shunned the Sweater Mafia and genuinely seemed into the party for Arianna. It looked like taking Kirstie down a peg had given Arianna a touch of legendary status around school that somehow they hadn't noticed until now.

The past few days, all those people looking, staring, in class, in study hall . . . this was why, Dawn realized. They were intimidated by Arianna. Interested and fascinated and dying to see what she'd do next.

"You're *popular*," Dawn said excitedly to Arianna. "Can you believe it?"

"Cool," Arianna said, still not quite looking at her. "Your sister here yet?"

Dawn frowned. "Not yet. You know Buffy, something's always coming up. But she promised—"

"Great," Arianna said, wandering off and joining the festivities.

Someone tapped Dawn on the shoulder. She turned and found herself looking into her sister's penitent face. Then she looked down at what Buffy was wearing—and was amazed.

"Do I look okay?" Buffy asked, indicating the effort she'd made in getting dressed up.

"Better than okay," Dawn said. "Major wow. Hey, you know that concert you were telling me about? I think you're right, I think I should go. . . ."

"Don't even try that one," Buffy said. "I was using it on Mom before you were even—"

"Hey, look who's here," Arianna said, strolling over on her mother's arm. Both were beaming—and Dawn knew for sure now that something was *very* wrong.

Buffy thought mother and daughter DuPrey looked simpatico. They gave off no signs of a history of anything more than good pals. Buffy tried to hide her surprise, but it was impossible. Arianna's forehead furrowed as she looked to Buffy, then to Dawn.

"You told her," Arianna said. "I don't have to be able to do anything special to be able to tell that."

*So Arianna's not using her powers,* Buffy thought. *I don't know if that's good or bad. . . .*

"No," Dawn said. "I mean, they weren't, I didn't mean—"

"Told who what?" Buffy asked, trying to cover for her sister.

"Arianna and I have had some problems," Mrs. DuPrey said, her voice smooth and sincere as she gazed at Buffy with predatory delight. "Truth to tell, I've been a lousy mother. Worse than that. But things are different now, and they're only going to get better."

Then the woman stepped back and merged with the crowd. "Arianna, I think we both know what happens now."

"Yes, Mother," Arianna said as the woman vanished again into the mass of people surrounding them. It was as if she were withdrawing to a safe distance. *Why?*

Arianna nodded at Buffy. "All black. Looks like you dressed for a funeral."

Buffy shot a desperate look at Dawn. "What am I missing here?"

"No, it's good," Arianna said. "Fitting."

"Pardon?" Buffy asked. Something was going on—but what?

Arianna leaned in close to Buffy. "Last night? That was my *father* you murdered. . . ."

"W-what?" Buffy said, pulling back fast, but not fast enough. Arianna's right hook smashed into her face so hard and so fast, the Slayer was down before she knew what was happening.

"No!" Dawn yelled as her sister hit the ground hard and didn't get up.

The music swelled, the rhythmic beat giving way to a mad, discordant swelter of ear-piercing, unearthly sound. Something was happening onstage. A swirling vortex of energy appeared, and dozens of inhuman creatures appeared, led by a fat, squat, scabrous demon.

"'No,'" the demon mused. "I just *love it* when they yell 'No'!"

With a nasty little laugh, Arianna lifted her chin. "Time to change into something more comfortable."

Dawn screamed as Arianna became a monster.

# Chapter Nineteen

From the stage, the squat demon in front of the infernal legion pointed at Arianna.

"I was a friend of your father's," the bloated demon said. He touched the silver spiral dangling from around his neck. "In his honor, I dedicate a new game. I call it *heads* and *spines*. The one who brings me the most, wins!"

Arianna had been told that an ally of her father would arrive and create a distraction to help her in her quest. That was why her mother had to leave when she did, so she would be safe from the dangers that were about to arrive. And . . . Arianna wasn't sure that she wanted her mother seeing her like this. That was foolish, considering the arrangement Mother had made with Father, to be . . . transformed.

*If being human means being away from you and your father, then I'd rather become something else,* Mother had told her. There was magic that could be worked to all but wipe away any vestige of their human appearance. But—did the woman really understand what that meant? To truly give up her humanity?

Arianna hoped her mother did—and that she did, as well. . . .

The Bronze exploded in chaos as demons of every size and shape leaped into the audience. Arianna saw Willow, Giles, and the others vault into the fray.

*Good,* Arianna thought. *That should keep the Scoobs away from here.*

She looked back to her small audience. The unmoving Slayer and her weeping sister. People chased by *things* surged around them.

"Arianna?" Dawn asked, staring in stark disbelief.

Bending low, Arianna nodded with satisfaction. This time, Arianna had control over the change. She had willed her body to transform a half dozen times today, preparing for this moment. The bloodlust was on her, yes, and she would need that, but her reason hadn't left her as it had last night.

Arianna stood in full demon form, the crimson dress in tatters at her clawed feet. She hadn't worn shoes this time, fully aware of what was going to happen.

Dawn backed away, shaking and sucking in rapid gasps of air as if she was about to have a fit.

"Try breathing," Arianna said, advancing on her, delighted that she could still speak despite her misshapen maw. "Inhale, exhale, *slowly.* Always works for me."

"Buffy," Dawn mewled, drawing the name out. *"Buff-eeeeeee!"*

Despite the pull of her human side, Arianna couldn't allow herself to care about Dawn's fear. It didn't matter now, none of it did. She had a job to do and she had to be strong, for Father. And that job was to reach down to where Buffy lay still and tear the Slayer's head off.

But the look in Dawn's eyes seized on her humanity and paralyzed her. Dawn would be left with no one, her mother gone, her sister killed before her eyes—

Dawn had been her friend. She deserved better.

"Look away," Arianna hissed.

"No," Dawn said, stopping suddenly, as if she'd guessed what Arianna meant to do. "Please, no . . ."

Arianna studied the way Dawn's gaze flickered between her and Buffy, the love, the terror, the need . . . the guilt?

Her instincts flared—and knowledge flooded into her, along with a towering rage.

"You were *using* me!" Arianna shrieked. "You wanted to get in and see what it was like to be one of the Scoobs. You wanted to make sure she couldn't keep you out!"

"Please," Dawn pleaded. "Arianna, you're my friend!"

Arianna stepped over Buffy's still form and laughed bitterly. "No, I'm a monster. A demon. You remember demons, right? Those things your sister kills?"

Dawn quaked in terror.

A phrase came to Arianna's mind, unbidden: *Blood. You can only trust your blood. Everyone else will betray you.*

"There's more to it," Dawn cried. "Please!"

"You're all the same!" Arianna said, hauling her taloned hand back to strike the scheming, wretched human *child* cowering before her.

Suddenly, a tiny, all too familiar blonde stepped between them.

"Damn, you're ugly," Buffy said.

Arianna roared and brought her talon down as Buffy leaped back, a single claw ripping open the front of her dress but not breaking skin. The Slayer dropped and swept Arianna's legs out from under her with a single kick. She hit the floor hard, only dimly aware that all the other demons were giving her a wide berth, leaving a small circle of open floor for their battle.

She saw the monstrosities, their razor-sharp pincers, sucking wounds with jagged teeth for faces, and laughing skulls wreathed with fire. She felt their bloodlust, their desire for suffering and death, little more.

Friends? Her father had been friends with *these?* How was that possible?

Ahead, she saw Buffy grab Dawn and push her toward the crowd.

"It's Arianna," Dawn hollered. "Buffy, that thing, it's—"

"I know! I'll deal with it."

*Like you dealt with my father?* Arianna thought, her rage clouding her reason. Screaming with rage, Arianna flew at them as Buffy shoved Dawn deep into the crowd. Arianna soared through the air, talons slashing, her maw wide and ready to tear out their *throats!*

Arianna landed on a pair of leather-clad demons with twisting ivory horns who had gotten in her way, her talons slashing into the bodies of the monsters as she crashed into them and dragged them down with her weight and momentum. She heard the Slayer, but didn't see her, as she struggled to her feet and saw two more of Buffy's friends approach.

"Wil, Tara, do whatever it takes, don't let anything happen to her!" Buffy commanded, handing her sister off to protectors.

*Wise move,* Arianna thought. *You're the one I want, anyway.*

Arianna rose to her full inhuman height and saw above the crowd. She spotted a bobbing blonde head breaking from a redhead and a pair of brunettes and brushed everyone aside as she loped toward her prey.

She'd tossed a dozen humans and three other demons out of her way when the crowd parted and she had the blonde cornered near the door.

It was Kirstie. Wrong blonde.

She was about to turn from her former tormentor when thoughts of all the misery Kirstie had inflicted on her and so many others overwhelmed her. Thoughts of revenge against this one shouldn't have mattered at this point; they were firmly rooted in her human side. But Buffy wouldn't run away now that she understood what was between Arianna and herself. Arianna didn't need to use her intuitive power to sense that much.

Opening her maw, she advanced as the leader of the Sweater Mafia shrieked and shrank before her in horror.

*Why not,* Arianna thought. She was a demon. In ways, they both were. . . .

Buffy found a clear path to the space off to the right of the stage. She rushed for it—and heard a pair of demons gaining on her.

Hands over her head, she performed a perfect handspring, vaulting into a forward flip. She grabbed at her dress's conservative slit in mid-flip and, pulling on it hard, the fabric ripped clear up to her hip. Another flip and she kicked off the shoes.

Now she could move. Landing hard, Buffy sprinted toward an old band poster, easily outpacing her pursuers.

Another demon leaped down from the stage. The female mist-wraith from the other night, a brand-new spiral-edged staff in her hands. *Wonderful.*

Suddenly, another form burst from the shadows, platinum hair, a swirling black leather coat rising like a cape. With a fearsome howl he took the mist-wraith by surprise, kicked the staff out of her hands, and drove a heavy steel spike through her chest. She dropped, clutching at the wound, as the staff rolled and flopped to Buffy's feet. She grabbed it and swung at the demons closing in from behind her. A pair of ichor-spurting bodies fell seconds before their severed heads dropped down beside them.

Buffy turned, the staff's bloody blade level and dripping with gore. "What are you doing here?"

"You're bloody well welcome, little miss all prepared for battle without your good buddy Spike!"

Buffy tossed him the staff, then tore the tacky painting from the wall, revealing an empty space with a satchel stuffed inside. She hauled it out and started grabbing weapons.

"Not exactly unprepared," Buffy said.

"Ah, yeah. This place does get beat up a lot, now dunnit?"

Buffy strapped knives to her thighs, throwing stars to her arms, and drew out the battle-ax she hadn't used since the night she'd saved Arianna's life at the Quick Stop.

"Hot dress, by the way," Spike said. "Like all the leg and cleavage."

"Willow and Tara are out there somewhere with Dawn. *Help them.*"

Spike's smug grin faded. Nodding, he raced into the rapidly thinning crowd.

Willow cast a sleep spell, taking out another demon. She was backed into a far corner, Tara and Dawn a few feet away, crouched behind an overturned table, barely fending off another attacker.

She tapped the brutish, scaly, fishy smelling demon on the shoulder. It hissed and reached for her, but she sent it off to fuzzy ol' land of Nod with a word and a gesture, then she helped Tara and Dawn out from hiding.

"Quick question," Tara said. "How long have you

been able to do that, and if you teach me, could we just put all these things to sleep before anyone else gets hurt?"

Willow frowned, searching for the exit where she'd seen Giles helping people escape. "Usually doesn't work unless these guys are, like, *really dumb,* or already under someone else's influence.

Tara gestured at the trio of demons Willow had already taken out.

"Right, yeah, it *does* work on these guys, so who cares why," Willow said. "Me with the hows and whys and not so much with the—"

"Look out!" Tara screamed.

Willow turned and saw a dark, ugly, pig-like face with a ring in its nose. She heard a crack and felt a splitting pain in her skull. She thought she heard Tara screaming her name, and Dawn just plain screaming.

Then there was another explosion of pain, and she wasn't thinking anything at all.

Anya sighed happily as she helped Xander herd screaming teenagers toward the kitchen and out the back door.

"I know I'm gonna regret asking this," Xander said, eyeing his beloved, "but I gotta know. Exactly what part of all this craziness is giving you a happy?"

"Nostalgia," Anya said, smiling and a little embarrassed. She grabbed a girl and gave her a little shove. "There you go. Through the door, not into the wall. Good little shrieking adolescent."

"Nostalgia?" Xander said. "Happy, fuzzy memories of mass carnage performed at the request of a fifteen-year-old who'd just been dumped?"

"No, silly!" Anya said, elbowing a jock who wasn't leaving room for anyone else to get away. "Back in the sixties, *The Ed Sullivan Show,* the Beatles playing live. One happy little vengeance demon with a backstage all-access pass and this hunky security guy who had the cutest little butt—"

"Always forgetting the slightly different perspective because of the nine hundred years of ancient history part, aren't I?"

She nodded gravely. He did that a lot, but she forgave him.

"At least there was no death or carnage," Xander said.

A rumbling voice said, "Night's young."

The screaming got worse as a demon rushed the exit.

The demon's flesh was Incredible Hulk green with black jagged stripes. He had one eye, a chain-mail frock, and a really nasty case of acne. He was also wide enough in the chest to fit two Xanders.

Anya dumped the punch bowl over his head. He turned, startled, his single eye blinking wildly. He roared, loosing a blast of concussive energy that hit Anya mid-chest and sent her careening back.

Fighting his way against the tide of escapees, Xander snatched up a metal folding chair and smashed it into the demon's stomach. It clanged against the mail and bounced off.

"Ah, no," Xander said.

The demon's meaty green hand closed around Xander's neck and lifted him off the ground.

A clang rang out as Anya smacked the back of the demon's skull with an appetizer tray. He didn't drop Xander. Instead, he turned his head and opened his mouth again.

"Stooges, don't fail me now," Xander said.

Xander thrust two fingers of each hand right at the demon's lone eye. A horrible sploosh and a deep rumbling scream echoed through the kitchen as he dropped Xander and went stumbling off, his hands closed over his wounded eye.

"Come on," Xander said. "Don't tell me you didn't see that one coming!"

Anya found a frying pan, beat the demon into unconsciousness, and rushed to Xander, her hands closing on the side of his face, her lips pressing against his.

*The teenagers seemed to be doing just fine,* she thought, drawing him close.

Dawn drew back as the pig-faced demon grabbed at her with his three-fingered, greasy hands.

"Sever the links," he said dully. "She must sever the links. . . ."

Tara was about to throw herself at the monster when Spike lightly brushed her aside.

"Let me, luv." He grabbed the thick-bodied pig-thing's wrist and twisted it in a sharp one-eighty. Bones crackled, and the demon squealed in agony. "Wanted to see if you'd do that."

Then Spike kicked it square in the neck, crushing its throat. The creature fell back, a limp, tubby sack of *very* dead demon. He glanced around for more attackers, then turned to Dawn. "You okay, sweet pea?"

Dawn nodded.

Tara was on her knees, cradling Willow. "She's out cold, but I think she's gonna be all right." Tara frowned. "Did you hear what that demon was saying? Willow said one of her spells usually only worked if a demon was under someone else's control. I get the feeling someone's controlling all these demons, but that doesn't make any sense if this is really part of the whole demon sports thing."

"I think I see your point, luv," Spike said. "If they're

brains are dulled, we might be able to take 'em down more easily. And there's a mystery here as to the how and why. But we've got a few more pressing issues in front of us now." He nodded to Willow. "Think you could drag her, carry her, whatever?"

Tara nodded.

"Good," Spike said. "I'm probably gonna need my hands free to get us through that lot by the—"

Dawn looked up to see why Spike had stopped.

A half dozen demons had broken from their attack on the fleeing party-goers and were running their way.

"Tara," Spike said evenly, "if you know any nice wakey-wakey-Willow-in-a-hurry, damn-the-consequences spells, I'm thinking now's the time."

With a roar, he launched himself at their attackers.

Giles lowered the sword he'd taken from a low level chaos demon and used it to split its skull. The Bronze was thinning out, and the remaining demons that had been tearing at the people trying to escape near his exit had gone unfocused suddenly and pulled away from the bevy of fresh kills still available to them.

Across the Bronze, he saw Buffy fighting several other demons attempting to reach the humans by Xander's and Anya's exit. The tall, charcoal-skinned demoness had disappeared somewhere around the main entrance.

Willow, Tara, Dawn . . . where were they?

Suddenly, he saw them, Spike somehow managing to keep a half dozen demons at bay while Tara and Dawn crouched over a fallen Willow.

He raised his sword, but his head was still swimming from the torrent of literally maddening energies the chaos demon had released with its death cry. He'd put up a spell of protection, but it had been just a little late.

Leaning against the wall, desperately trying to regain his full senses, Giles glanced to the stage.

Verdelot stood there, his grotesque head raised as he took in the madness with an odd look of concern. Something was clearly troubling him. *What could it be?*

A figure stood behind him, off to the shadows.

It was Arianna's mother. Willow had pointed her out to him earlier. She was speaking to Verdelot, her hands waving urgently. Whatever troubled him, affected her, too.

His head cleared, and he pushed away from the wall. This mystery would have to wait. He ran toward the cluster of demons who were quickly beating Spike down.

It was time for Ripper to pay a visit.

Arianna returned to the battle, angry, frustrated, and shaken. Father had been right. She needed infinitely more training and experience.

Little tufts of blond hair were lodged in her talons. She hadn't hurt Kirstie *much*. Really, she'd only scared the daylights out of her and given the ruler of that clique a new haircut.

That hadn't been what had cost her so much time. The horned demons she'd accidentally wounded came back for her, attacking with a murderous frenzy. Strangely, they looked as if they had just woken from a dream and were now struggling to make sense of where they were and their exact purpose. *Why would that be?*

As she fought them, Arianna felt her strength grow, her power rise, and now she was anxious to face her true enemy for the last time. But where was the Slayer?

"Hey, Miss Nastypants," Buffy called from the now otherwise empty stage. "Wanna play?"

Arianna roared, crackling energy racing through her powerful demon body.

* * *

Buffy leaped from the stage, her double ax flashing, as Arianna raced at her. The beast that had been her friend vaulted—and missed the Slayer by a mile.

"That the best you can do?" Buffy asked with a joviality she didn't really feel, hefting the ax.

Arianna landed hard, sliding and crashing into the base of the stage. Reaching beneath it, she smiled horribly.

"I was here earlier, too," Arianna said, retrieving her father's sword from where she must have hidden it beneath the stage. "I wanted this handy."

"How nice for you," Buffy said. "Quick question: Any chance we can talk about this?"

Arianna swung the sword easily now, as if she'd been born to it.

Buffy jumped back, away from its silvery arc. "Taking that as a 'no.'"

Grabbing the sword hilt in both hands, Arianna drove an upper thrust at Buffy's heart. Buffy countered using her double ax, cutting from above to block Arianna's blade.

"Have to talk to Wil about that checking-for-demon-blood spell," Buffy said.

*Keep the banter light,* Buffy thought. She had to keep Arianna distracted while she bought herself enough time to come up with some way to get through to her.

Buffy turned her body away as Arianna swung the blade hard at Buffy's arm, then countered by slicing her double ax across the cracked flesh of Arianna's cheek. Both warriors withdrew, circling, scanning for an opening.

"Looks like you still need some training," Buffy said. "Lesson one, when your enemy's lying dazed and helpless at your feet, don't waste time getting into it with the kid sister. I know she can be annoying, but really, think about it."

"You're trying to distract me," Arianna said. "Or make me lose it and do something stupid. Human tactics. But I'm not human, not anymore!"

Buffy refused to believe that, despite Arianna's hideous appearance.

Arianna feinted with the sword and Buffy whirled fast, bringing the biting edge of the double ax down upon the weapon. Steel clanged, and sparks pinwheeled in the darkened club. Arianna struck with her left talon, raking across Buffy's shoulder, and Buffy turned with the force of the blow, fell, and lashed out with a hard kick to Arianna's ankle.

Suddenly, Arianna was off-balance, the sword threatening to leave her grip as she plummeted to the floor. Buffy saw her gaze went to the weapon, clearly the only thing Arianna had left of her father. The transformed teenager's entire focus seemed to go right to the sword, to not let it slip from her grasp as she struck the ground.

That gave Buffy an opening. She grabbed Arianna's left wrist and hauled it up behind her, planting a foot in the small of the girl's back.

"She'll kill me," Arianna whispered. "Father, I've failed you!"

Buffy's lips curled in disgust. Arianna thought she would just kill her? She crouched to whisper in her captive's ear.

"Lesson two," Buffy said. "I'm not your enemy."

With an inhuman cry, Arianna sprang to her feet and threw herself back, smashing Buffy against the stage. Buffy grunted with pain and slid to the floor as Arianna turned and raised her sword.

"Liar! You're all liars!" Arianna bellowed. She brought the sword down, and Buffy jumped out of the way easily and leaped to the stage as Arianna launched after her. Buffy evaded every thrust of Arianna's sword without so much as a single parry.

"Listen to me!" Buffy yelled. "All I know is, last night I'm on patrol, minding my own business, and this guy comes out of nowhere, swinging that sword, trying to take my head off."

"You want to kill us all!" Arianna said, swinging the weapon high. "You've been our enemy all along!"

Buffy tumbled low and flipped from the stage. She stood, weapon raised, as Arianna leaped after her.

"No," Buffy said. "I was defending myself. Sometimes, I'm protecting others. That's what Slayers do."

Their battle was met, steel on steel.

"My people need a hero," Arianna said. "The Reaver's their only hope!"

"So that's you? I slay, you reave? Only it's big bad scary *human beings* giving you problems? Please."

"You don't understand. None of you do!"

Their weapons collided again.

"Arianna, it doesn't have to be like this!"

"Your death is all that will bring Father back," Arianna snarled, attacking with a renewed frenzy.

Arianna fought hard but sensed she was losing. Buffy's thrusts and swings had become more complex, harder to anticipate—

*Power, you're not using your power!* Arianna screamed at herself. *Read her, who cares what you might find out, read her before it's too late!*

Arianna tried to use her power, but . . . something was blocking her. She felt the force of another will upon her, somehow tempering her abilities. Was it the witch, Willow? She had a sense that it was not. *Who, then?*

*And what was it that person didn't want her to know?*

Buffy swung the double ax, and Arianna grabbed one of the Bronze's tables, narrowly raising it in time to use it as a shield. The force of the blow buried the ax head deep in the wood. And stuck there.

"Ugh," Buffy said.

With a roar of triumph, Arianna thrust the table at Buffy, smashing it upon her before the Slayer could get out of the way. She kicked the Slayer and heard her moan as her body flipped out from the wreckage, her weapon sliding from her hands. Buffy's head lolled, and she lay still and vulnerable.

*I won't hesitate again,* Arianna promised herself. *I won't! Hesitation is a human trait and I'm beyond such things now. I have to be!*

Arianna raised her weapon for the killing blow—and a voice stopped her.

"You have no idea what you're becoming, do you?"

Arianna turned slightly to see a man standing before her, a blood-drenched human with shattered glasses, tattered clothing.

Giles.

Buffy's watcher stood his ground, knowing full well that Arianna could strike him down, cut him in half with her talons or the sword. But she didn't. A part of her was obviously still clinging to her humanity, and Giles had to appeal to that part if he was to save Buffy.

"I'm the Reaver," Arianna said. "Champion of my people."

"The Reaver, is it?" Giles asked with a raised eyebrow. "And is it the Reaver's job to usher in the darkness? To hold back the light? Because by killing her, that's what you'll be helping to do. Yet Buffy said you wanted to be a hero."

"I will be a hero, to my kind."

"Demons."

"We're different, not evil."

"Prove it!" Giles said. "The Slayer is a preserver. If you kill her, then the Reaver's nothing but another destroyer. You're half-demon. That means you're half-human, too. You're free to choose your destiny."

Suddenly, Verdelot approached. "Don't let them distract you with their lies! Honor your father. Become what you know in your heart you wish to become!"

Giles heard Buffy stirring and saw Arianna turn to her. The moment was almost gone.

Verdelot raised a dagger and surged forward, aiming the weapon at Giles's heart before he had a chance to defend himself.

Then, a sharp steel spike was suddenly at Verdelot's lumpy, fleshy throat.

"Not so fast, bouncing boy," Spike said, edging the weapon closer. "This one's been blessed by a thousand holy virgins. A tiny prick of the skin and a thing like you is done for, mate."

"Bluffing," Verdelot hissed.

"Try me," Spike said. "No, I mean it. Please. I love to see your kind go all puffy and explode."

Giles looked back at Buffy and Arianna—and his blood chilled as he realized what Buffy was going to do . . . and that there was nothing he could do to stop her.

"Arianna."

She whirled. Buffy was on one knee before her, her hands open, weaponless. Arianna cast a quick glance about the Bronze. The place was clear, the party-goers gone, and Verdelot's legions either dead or otherwise indisposed, while the Scoobs crowded around Buffy. Dawn was there, tears streaming down her cheeks.

"Game time's over," Willow said weakly, clinging to Tara for support. "And I don't think any of this is what it looked like. Think about it, Arianna. Why would the demons Verdelot brought with him run when there was still a game to be played, a prize to be won? And why didn't any of them try to kill Buffy?"

"Yeah," Tara said. "It was as if they were being controlled, right from the start. . . ."

Arianna stood trembling, needing both hands to clutch her father's sword. She knew what she was. How she could take them all!

Buffy looked up at her sadly. "I just wanted to keep you from all this. I didn't want you to have to—"

"It's a trick," Arianna said, staring down at the weaponless Slayer. "You're just trying to get me close enough because you've got something planned."

Buffy shook her head solemnly. "No."

Arianna wished her mother were near. Though she knew her mother had left earlier, she looked beyond her opponents, anyway, scanning for any sign of the woman. She needed someone who understood. . . .

"If you're looking for your mother, she left a few moments ago," Giles said, a note of disgust in his voice.

"How . . . ," Arianna asked quietly.

"One doesn't need powers to understand what you're looking for." He nodded at Verdelot. "First, she was conspiring with this . . . thing. Then she ran when it looked as if things might not turn out exactly as you people had planned."

"Did she?" Verdelot muttered, flushing with anger. "I suppose I shouldn't be surprised."

Arianna was surprised. Mother *had* stayed? That means she had seen Arianna like this. Was that sight what had driven her off? Had she changed her mind about abandoning her humanity once she had seen what Arianna had become?

And why had she been with Verdelot?

Suddenly, Verdelot twisted away from Spike with surprising speed, the weapon ripping across his neck, opening his flesh, and leaving nothing but a small, black, bubbling wound that quickly faded.

"Hey, that wasn't a bluff!" Spike said, his face suddenly transforming, his forehead becoming bumpy, ridged, his teeth becoming sharp fangs. "You don't know all the spells I had to sit through just so I could hold the thing without getting hurt. Wot the bleedin' hell's goin' on here?"

"Wait," Arianna said. "You're . . . you're a vampire?"

"Funny, ennit? Both of us demons, of a sort. Only I've made the choice to play on the right side, girlie. Got my reasons, sure. But no one makes me do a bleedin' thing I don't want to do. Why is it I get the feelin' that's not the case with you?"

Arianna looked to Verdelot, who stared at the proceedings with what appeared to be growing alarm.

"He's right," Anya said. "I was a vengeance demon for nine hundred years. Becoming human again wasn't my choice, but what I've done with my humanity . . . that's been nobody's business but mine."

Arianna glanced down at Buffy. She was friends, or partners of sorts, with the vampire Spike? And Anya might as well have been another member of the Slayer's extended family.

But how could that be, if Buffy was truly the enemy?

Buffy saw Verdelot gesturing and was about to grab a weapon to stop his spellcasting when a pulsating wall of pure sparkling energy appeared, a blue-white dome surrounding Buffy, Arianna, and Verdelot. Instantly, Giles, Willow, and Tara set to work on bringing it down from the other side, but Buffy had a sense that their efforts would be too little, too late.

Arianna looked down at Buffy. "You murdered my father," Arianna said. "He's all I had, and you took him from me!"

Buffy's eyes were soft, compassionate, her hands still open and weaponless. "Do what you want. I won't fight you."

"Finish it, child," Verdelot urged. "All is in readiness. Be true to your blood and take the life of your father's slayer—only then can you bring him back from the fires of eternity."

Buffy drew a sharp breath as Arianna took a single step closer to her—and stopped.

"I told you before, no one gave me a choice," Buffy said, nodding at the sword in Arianna's hand. "I don't care what kind of hell that thing can send me to, it'd be worth it to keep the same thing from happening to someone else."

Arianna hesitated.

"I didn't know he was your father," Buffy said. "But even if I had, *he* attacked *me*. He tried to kill me. That's what demons do. A lot of them, anyway. It's one of the reasons I'm here. And if it were happening again *right now,* I'd do the same thing. I'd protect myself and I'd protect the innocent. That's what Slayers do."

Buffy caught Verdelot eyeing the wall of force anxiously. Already, a small point of darkness had appeared upon its surface, courtesy of Wil, Tara, and Giles.

"What is there to think about?" Verdelot asked. "Do it! Sever the link."

"Sever the link," Buffy repeated, certain she had heard the phrase before. Then it came to her, and she looked at Arianna. "These demons were under his control! Most of them were mumbling that same thing."

Arianna trembled, the sword inching higher in her

inhuman hands.

"You *have* power," Buffy continued. "Use it to look inside me and find out the truth, so you'll know you're making your own choices, so you'll have that freedom. You owe yourself that much."

Trembling, Buffy watched Arianna raise the sword even higher. "I'm your friend, Arianna. Believe it."

"Lies," Arianna whispered. "All lies!"

Arianna felt her strength rising as she hefted the weapon.

*If Buffy's lying, then it's easy enough to find out.*

She tried again to read Buffy, but the force that prevented her before acted upon her again—only this time it was weaker.

She did sense something, though, something that had nothing to do with Buffy. A being was approaching, someone who could pierce this sphere of force as if it were nothing.

"The Herald comes to offer you the third gift," Verdelot said. "Time is running out, child. Kill the Slayer and *sever* the *link* to your humanity!"

The tiny spot of darkness in Verdelot's wall widened. Arianna could hear shouts from without.

Buffy's gaze was unwavering. "I've been telling you all along, the choice is in your hands. Just make sure you can live with your decision."

Arianna's instinctual power flared, and this time, she fought the strange force that was keeping it down—and won.

She gasped. Buffy was telling the truth. The Slayer wouldn't fight her—and she didn't consider all demons the enemy. Buffy wasn't out to trick her by laying down her weapon; she would actually allow herself to be struck down if that's what it took to show Arianna the truth.

Verdelot raised his knife. "I'll do it, then!"

Arianna whirled and struck at Verdelot, the portly demon leaping back with a surprising speed and grace—considering his size—to avoid the swiftly falling blade.

No, not surprising. Impossible. He wasn't what he appeared to be.

"Know your enemies, child!" Verdelot hollered. "I'm not one of them!"

Arianna wasn't so sure. She trained her power on the demon lord, allowing the blood and chaos surrounding her to fall away. Sound and color drained, and a crisp, clear understanding replaced them.

Suddenly, she knew the man before her, knew him from his sweat, from the angle of his shoulders, from the distribution of his weight, from the rhythm of his very breath. She knew him in her blood. Her senses rushed back to her. "Father."

The glamour disguising him shattered before he could issue the slightest protest. The disgusting shell with which he had surrounded himself was gone, and the Marquis Aurek Kiritan stood revealed.

For an instant, Arianna wanted to run into his arms, to have him hold her and tell her everything would be all right, that she'd never be alone again.

The instant passed. He'd lied to her and arranged for all of this to happen.

Arianna's mind raced. She understood how it could be done: a spell to make someone else *look* like him last night, a willing or unwilling ally to sacrifice in the fight with the Slayer.

She'd been manipulated. Everything had been carefully timed and meticulously staged: the arrival of the scroll in her room; the amount of time it would take for her to reach the killing ground; the precise moment the double would attack—even her mother's newfound beauty and affection.

She thought of the thick curling root that she'd snagged with her shoe, the fall that had cost her precious seconds. She'd blamed herself for that delay, thinking it was a stupid, clumsy move on her part, rooted directly in her humanity. If she hadn't fallen, she might have stopped the battle.

Yet she was sure it hadn't been there. Now she knew the truth: The root had been a part of Father's plan, another tiny bit of magic cast to make it grab her leg at just the right instant and haul her down.

He must have been watching her last night. How many other times had he been there, just out of reach of her senses? How much of what she'd seen and done, how much of what she'd thought and felt, had he manipulated?

Arianna looked to her father through her crimson haze. *"Why?"*

"It was a test," Aurek said, fear and pure desperation radiating from him. "I *told* you: fealty. Following my commands without question, that is what is required for you to become the Reaver, to become our people's champion."

"No," Buffy said. "Not a champion. A tool to make him more powerful."

Aurek shook his head. "Arianna, your human blood is making you weak, making you question what you *know* to be true. You want this destiny—I can feel it! The Slayer and her sister are nothing to you. Renounce your feelings for them, sever the links in your mind if not in the flesh. Then the final gift can be yours!"

"Such a deal," Buffy said, getting to her feet and working the kinks out of her sore arms and legs. "I don't even have to die. You just have to promise you'll work real hard to be just like dear old dad, a psychotic, lying piece of—"

Aurek surged forward, backhanding Buffy so hard, she was sent flying to the edge of the mystic barrier—and beyond.

"We can leave the circle," Aurek said. "But only one can enter. The Herald bearing your final gift. Your birthright."

Arianna felt a fiery presence come into being behind her. She turned—and beheld the Herald.

Her mind registered his form as male, but, in truth, the Herald defied such categorization. The shape reconciled, burst apart, and remade itself in a thousand different forms, many so vast, she could not even comprehend their boundaries, as what appeared to be a single hand was raised toward her.

A voice that resonated with thunder and wrath entered her brain.

*"The power of the Reaver is your right by birth,"* the Herald said. *"Power to level worlds, to cause untold suffering. To unite the Seven Realms in terror and spread that darkness throughout each and every reality, even this one. You have only to take my hand. I am the doorway."*

Arianna stared at the shimmering invitation.

The Reaver was no hero. It was all lies.

"What are you waiting for?" Father screamed. "Idiot child, *do it!*"

Arianna dropped the sword.

The Herald nodded and withdrew, his shimmering light fading as he became mist and vanished.

Arianna felt a sudden weakness. She dropped to her knees, gasped, and saw that she was human once more.

Aurek snatched up his sword. "You would do this to me? Call him back! It may not be too late. Do it!"

"You're not my father," Arianna said. "One thing Mother didn't lie about. My father's dead—at least to me."

Aurek screamed, and Arianna hung her head, waiting.

"You're my chattel," Aurek said as he grabbed her hair with one hand, his sword with the other, and poised the blade at her throat. A single cut and it would be over.

Arianna was afraid, but not nearly so much as she expected. If only she could tell Buffy and Dawn how sorry she was. . . .

Aurek sneered. "It is my right to do with you what I will. You still have Kiritan blood in you, and that means power—whether you're the Reaver or not. I won't have you coming after me!"

*Coming after you*, Arianna thought. *That's the last thing I'd ever want to do.*

The muscles in Aurek's powerful arms tensed. Arianna wondered what the metal would feel like when it cut through her neck. A bitter chill? Or would it be hot, like a boiling river?

From the beginning, Buffy had been trying to make her see that she could live her life in whatever way made her happy, that she was free to choose. But Buffy hadn't known what was inside her.

She knew what she was, and she couldn't bear the thought of the horror inside her hurting anyone again.

She'd never tasted freedom. Not true freedom. Not until tonight.

It was worth dying for.

Arianna closed her eyes. She thought of the beautiful fortress city on the edge of the waterfall, the image from the cover of the book Dawn bought for her. Summoning all of her will, she tried to make it real.

It would be a warm, spring day, she decided, with a cool, comforting breeze. The rush of water would be the city's pulse, the beautiful garden of miracles she had glimpsed in dreams its heart. Amazing sights and smells filled her imagination. She was ready. "Do it," she whispered.

With a laugh, he obliged her.

The mystical barrier fell as Aurek drew the blade across his daughter's throat, sending her convulsing and clutching her neck as she collapsed facedown, a small pool of blood spilling out and dampening her golden hair. Buffy screamed as she leaped at him, the double ax smashing at his face, blocked by his bloody sword.

Buffy crashed into the demon, sending both of them sprawling to the ground. She heard Dawn screaming, saw the others rushing to Arianna's side.

Buffy vaulted to her feet.

He raised his hand, his fingers beginning an arcane gesture.

Buffy whirled with the double ax, and his hand went one way, the rest of the shrieking demon the other.

It wasn't enough, not nearly enough. Buffy rushed him, easily blocking his clumsy swordplay, her weapon ripping through his armor, burying itself in his dark flesh. His mouth opened, as if to cast another spell, and his eyes, glowing red coals of pure hatred, brightened into flares.

"You wanna lose the tongue?" Buffy hissed. "One syllable."

He closed his mouth and fought her off as best he could. She kicked his knee, shattering it, bringing him down. His blade came around, and she knocked it from his grasp with little effort. He lunged at her like the insane, wounded animal that he was, the ferocity of his attack surprising Buffy, giving him a split second advantage. She went down, feeling his burning hand on her leg, tearing away the Velcro knife strap and the weapons it held.

Bounding back to her feet, she brought the ax down just as the sharpest of the daggers appeared in his hand.

This time, she didn't stop at the hand.

Bone cracked, and blood splattered as his arm fell away from his body. Shrieking in agony, Aurek fell back, shuddering, luminous blue tears of pain streaking his inhuman face.

Buffy raised the ax with both hands.

"No!" Giles shouted.

She heard Dawn cry out. *"Buffy!"*

The demon writhed on the floor, and Buffy felt the muscles in her arms burning, screaming for release.

"Don't kill him," Willow said. "Not with Dawn here, not like this."

Buffy's chest was heaving. She clutched the double ax so hard, her hand *ached*.

The witch smiled, her eyes pure black. "I've got something better."

Aurek Kiritan was only barely aware of what was happening to him. The humans were preparing something, the child with the crimson hair using odd phrases like "Drawing Back the Veils" and "Tracing back the last big spells this guy did" and "Finding a back door into the system, sending in a worm."

Meaningless. Completely meaningless. The fools had let him live. His limbs would regenerate, and his strength would return. Given time, he would be whole again . . . then he would know vengeance.

Suddenly, as mystical energies rose about him, he heard his own words.

*I can unhinge your soul and send it screaming into the Vast for all eternity.*

An empty threat he'd directed at the true Verdelot.

Such a thing wasn't possible. Not unless—

A vortex formed about him, and suddenly he was on the Rainbow Bridge, the Road Eterna, staring at a vista far more terrible than any he had ever imagined to the side of the path.

The Vast. The dawning of all things. The primordial chaos that was life, death, eternity, and damnation.

A short, bitter laugh sounded behind him.

"What—" Aurek began as *something* grabbed him by the neck of his armor and hauled him into the air. He glimpsed one of the dark, almost faceless guardians he had bested to gain passage to the human realm.

Then he was tossed, headlong, into the endless torment of the dimension called the Vast.

His screams would be a symphony for eternity.


Arianna trembled, her hand glowing bright blue as it slid away from the cut across her throat.

She recalled her surprise that the sword's kiss had been so light, felt the surprise pouring off her father as he stepped away from her in mid-cut.

*You still have Kiritan blood in you. That means power, whether you're the Reaver or not.*

Like the power of healing . . .

Arianna rolled onto her side, hearing a short, sharp gasp from the young woman beside her.

Dawn stared down at her in wonder. She tried to speak, tried to say Arianna's name, tried to say so many things.

Arianna knew. She could feel what was in Dawn's heart. Words weren't needed.

She took the girl's hand and smiled.

Then the others were coming. Someone was yelling for Buffy as Xander's sweater was slipped over Arianna's head, allowing her to revel in its warmth. She felt hands on her and arms around her.

Their touch, their love . . . the freedom they had granted her and helped her grant herself . . .

It was the first breath of a new life.

Soon, Buffy had Arianna on her feet. The others helped her as they left, sirens blaring in the distance.

"This was just like going to Disneyland," Xander said as the night air struck them all.

Buffy looked at him. "Um-hmmm?"

"In that I've been there and never want to go back."

Buffy saw Arianna and Dawn walking with their arms around each other. She took a deep breath of the bracing air and felt Giles's hand on her shoulder. Spike was skulking somewhere far behind them, shrouded in shadows. He did come in handy sometimes.

"By the by," Giles said. "Dawn mentioned something about a concert earlier."

"Not you, too," Buffy said, moaning.

"Perhaps it's something she and Arianna could do together," Giles said. "There is no greater gift than freedom. Particularly the freedom to make your own choices. You know that."

Those two, a fifteen- and a sixteen-year-old at some lunatic concert. Buffy tried to picture it—then realized she'd never say yes if she did. "Get me the 411, we'll talk," Buffy said.

"Word up, then," Giles said brightly.

She stared at her mentor as if he'd just been possessed.

He smiled and gave her a hug. "I love to see that look on your face, Buffy. It lets me know you're alive."

Deep inside, that's how she felt. Alive—

And free.

* * *

It was late when Arianna got home. Mother was up, waiting. She told Mother what had happened to Aurek, then stood back and waited.

"That's it, then," Arianna's mother said. With trembling hands she reached up to her face, only to find the glow of youth was gone, her skin pale, drawn, and wrinkled once more. She looked ten, possibly twenty years older than she should have. The hate in her heart was again visible as she twisted her features into a mask of roaring agony. "You *worthless* little piece of *trash*. You took it away. You *took* it all *away!*"

Arianna slowly turned to face the woman.

"You don't have anything to say? I should have gotten *rid* of you a long time ago, but I thought he'd come back if I had something of his, I thought he would, and he did! But you . . . you idiot! You pathetic little nothing, you—"

A scream burst from Arianna's lungs, and she *changed*—into something new. Suddenly, she was beautiful.

She knew that her body was statuesque, the human ideal of pure perfection. Waves of black hair whipped about her lovely features and reached down to cover her nakedness. Her flesh was a luminous midnight blue, polished and smooth and flowing like glass under a flame. Her exquisite eyes burned like fireflies in amber, and her hands were long and graceful, powerful, but human. Arianna's mother was frozen in terror.

"Things are going to change," Arianna said in a voice that was haunting and heartbreaking in its splendor, a commanding voice that would never need to be sullied with rage, never raised in anger. "I understand that I can't have what I wanted from you. You don't know what it means to love."

Arianna reached out and sank her hand into the solid wall, clawing through the concrete with effort. Much of the strength she'd possessed was gone. Not all.

"I know what I am now," Arianna said. "I'm more

than you'll ever be."

The woman quaked as Arianna took a single step closer and stopped. She closed her eyes, and willed her human form to return. Her flesh became soft and fully human once more, but the confidence, the way she held herself, the power in her eyes as she opened them and fixed the woman with them—it was the same.

"We may live under the same roof for the next few years, but it'll be on my terms, not yours. I'm through caring about what you think and what you want and what you believe is right. It ends here and now."

"S-sweetheart—" the woman quaked, taking another step back and tripping over debris. She fell hard, and Arianna made no move to help her. Instead, Arianna stared at her with something worse than loathing or contempt. She looked at the woman as if she weren't there, as if she had never truly been there at all.

She felt *nothing* as her mother crawled a few feet, lifted herself up, and trembled off into the shadows.

It was where she belonged.

# Chapter Twenty

A week had passed since the knock-down, drag-out at the Bronze. Buffy was taking a rare day off. Just a little time to get a facial, wander around, hit the shops, swing by the mall. Normal stuff.

Human stuff.

She was on the mall's second floor, near a dress shop, when she heard Dawn's unmistakable *honk-snuff-snuff* of a laugh. It was followed by a gaggle of giggles. The next store over was a bookstore. *The* bookstore, actually. Arianna had gotten her first job there, and seemed to be having the time of her life.

Buffy eased around the corner and chanced a look inside. Dawn, Arianna, Melissa, and a couple of girls Buffy didn't recognize were gathered around a display of romance novels. Dawn had one open. *Caribbean Blues,* the cover declared.

"Okay, this one's perfect," Dawn said. "Check this. 'Gunther ravished her with his gaze. "Come to me," he *oiled.* She reluctantly obeyed. . . .'"

The cloudburst of giggles opened up again.

Melissa handed Arianna a book. "This is fun. Why don't you try?"

Arianna seemed a little hesitant. Buffy knew trust was not something that would ever come easily to Arianna, not after all she'd been through.

This was the hand of friendship, though. It was being offered without anything attached.

All Arianna had to do was take it.

Buffy bit her lip. *Come on, come on,* she cheered inwardly. *You can do it, come on. . . .*

Arianna took the book with trembling hands, then she calmed and opened to a page at random. In a ridiculous voice that reminded Buffy of the swashbuckling Spaniard from the *Princess Bride,* Arianna said, "'Fernando, you must take her to your hideaway and have your vile will upon her. It is the only way to *relieve* the swelling burden her beauty puts upon you. . . .'"

The girls nearly fell over laughing this time.

Melissa rubbed Arianna's arm and said, "That's classic! You can pick 'em!"

"You go, girl!" the other one said. Then she frowned. "Wait, do people still say that?"

They laughed again, and this time, Arianna was laughing with them. Melissa and the new pair took off quickly, leaving Dawn and Arianna. Buffy was about to leave, but Arianna's words stopped her.

"What if they knew?" Arianna asked. "Y'know, that I'm different."

"Who isn't?" Dawn asked.

Her simple words seemed to melt Arianna's fears. She smiled—and hugged Dawn for the first time. Dawn hugged her back, and they looked like two souls taking shelter from a storm that could never touch them so long as they were together. Friends, now and forever.

Smiling, Buffy left Arianna to her new life.

# ABOUT THE AUTHOR

Scott Ciencin is a *New York Times* best-selling author of adult and children's fiction. Praised by *Science Fiction Review* as "one of today's finest fantasy writers" and listed in the *Encyclopedia of Fantasy*, Scott has written over fifty novels and many short stories and comic books. His most recent work is the novelization of *Jurassic Park III* for Random House and *Survivor*, the first in a series of original *Jurassic Park* adventures for young readers. He is currently working on *Anakin Skywalker: A Jedi's Journal*, the *Angel* novel *Vengeance* (coauthored with Dan Jolley) and several original properties.